Attack on the Tower of London

Roy MacGregor

An M&S Paperback Original from
McClelland & Stewart Ltd.
The Canadian Publishers

For Brent Munroe, 1948–2004, who taught us all to nourish the child inside.

The author is grateful to Doug Gibson, who thought up this series, and to Alex Schultz, who pulls it off.

Copyright © 2004 by Roy MacGregor

Library and Archives Canada Cataloguing in Publication

MacGregor, Roy, 1948-
    Attack on the Tower of London / Roy MacGregor.

(The Screech Owls series ; 19)
ISBN 0-7710-5648-6

I. Title. II. Series: MacGregor, Roy, 1948- . Screech Owls series ; 19.

PS8575.G84A67 2004   jC813'.54   C2004-902381-0

We acknowledge the financial support of the Government of Canada through the Book Publishing Industry Development Program and that of the Government of Ontario through the Ontario Media Development Corporation's Ontario Book Initiative. We further acknowledge the support of the Canada Council for the Arts and the Ontario Arts Council for our publishing program.

Cover illustration by Gregory C. Banning
Typeset in Bembo by M&S, Toronto
Printed and bound in Canada

McClelland & Stewart Ltd.
The Canadian Publishers
481 University Ave.
Toronto, Ontario
M5G 2E9
www.mcclelland.com

2 3 4 5 6   09 08 07 06 05

TRAVIS LINDSAY HAD NO SENSE OF PASSING OUT.

Had it been presented to him as an option – "Look, kid, you can either keep staring at this grisly sight or you can be unconscious" – he would have happily volunteered to black out and crash to the floor in front of the rest of the Screech Owls.

But he'd had no choice whatsoever in the matter.

One moment Travis was staring at the naked, bloodied body swinging from the rope, its desperately clawing hands tied behind its back, and the next moment he was sinking into oblivion, darkness drawing over him like a welcome comforter.

He could take no more of the Chamber of Horrors.

Travis was not aware of Muck and Mr. Dillinger grabbing him and carting him off to the first-aid room. He did not see his so-called best friend, Nish, snickering so hard it seemed his big tomato of a face was going to explode. He did not know that Sarah Cuthbertson, too, had staggered, and would have gone down had Sam and Fahd not grabbed her.

And he certainly did not hear the tall woman in the uniform say, "It happens all the time," her red lipstick splash of a smile seeming horribly out of place in a room where a beaten and naked man was swinging from a rope, where bloodied heads were on display beside the terrible contraption that had lopped them off, and where, to the sounds of agonizing screams and creaking machinery, a heavy wheel was crushing the very life out of a nearly naked young man with long flowing hair.

Travis had felt fine as the tour guide for Madame Tussaud's waxworks museum took the team through the rooms filled with look-alike figures of movie and rock stars – he'd borrowed Data's digital camera to take a shot of Nish with Nish's great hero, Elvis Presley – and he'd been fine as Muck lingered over all those boring figures from history like Napoleon and Horatio Nelson and more kings and queens than you'd find in a pocketful of British change.

And he had even been okay, if barely, when they first entered the Chamber of Horrors and heard the spine-tingling, gut-wrenching sound effects rising from the corner where the young man was being tortured on the wheel.

He'd survived a look at Vlad the Impaler, the first figure on display as the Screech Owls had

2

crowded into the eerily lit room. He'd listened patiently as the tour guide calmly explained how old Vlad used to get his kicks out of tossing women and children onto sharpened stakes and laughing as they slowly died. He'd looked, not once, but twice, at the longhaired, moustachioed ruler as he stood by a bloodied stake holding up a severed head like it was some trophy bass he'd just caught.

He'd survived a peek at Joan of Arc, the pretty teenager burning at the stake, and all the various kindly-looking British murderers who used to do nasty things, such as drown their wives in acid baths or brick them into their kitchen walls.

He had even coped with the realistic sight of Madame Tussaud herself as she stood in a Paris graveyard, a lantern raised in one hand as she searched for the severed head of Marie Antoinette so she could capture the French queen's surprised look just as the guillotine fell.

But Guy Fawkes he could not handle.

In all his life, in all his many nightmares, Travis had never seen a sight so horrific. The body of Fawkes hung from a rope – his naked skin slashed by knives and whips, his hands tied behind his back – as his dark-bearded executioner regarded him with stern delight.

The sight had been bad enough, but the tour guide's description of Fawkes – spoken in a lovely English accent that might as well have been talking about floral arrangements – had been the final straw.

"You come from Canada, where you celebrate something called Hallowe'en, I believe . . ."

"Just had it!" shouted Fahd.

"Yes, well, in this country we have Guy Fawkes Day, which will happen later this week. It's sort of like your Hallowe'en. There will be bonfires all over Britain on the night of November 5, all in memory of this gentleman you see here swinging from the rope . . ."

"No way!" said Derek.

"Guy Fawkes was hanged in the year 1606 – that's about four hundred years ago – after he and several other men were caught plotting to blow up the Houses of Parliament. He was, many say, the world's first terrorist. And to set an example to anyone else who might be thinking of committing such an act, he was given the most awful punishment imaginable. The hanging you see here was the *gentle* part of it . . ."

"Sick!" said Sam.

"Very sick," the guide said, her lipstick smiling. "Guy Fawkes was sentenced by the British courts to be hanged, drawn, and quartered. He would be hanged until almost dead – this is what we have on display here at Madame Tussaud's – and then, while he was still barely alive, they would take a sword and disembowel him, burning his entrails before his face as he was forced to watch.

"The last sensation he would ever feel would be the executioner's broadaxe coming down upon his neck."

"*I'M GONNA HURL!*" Nish shouted out, laughing like a maniac.

The tour guide held up a long finger, with a perfectly manicured nail at its tip.

"That would not be the end of it," she said, still smiling primly. "Even after his head was cut off, the punishment would continue. His body would be quartered by tying the arms and legs to four workhorses and driving them in four different directions until it split into pieces – that's what they mean by 'hanged, drawn, and quartered' – and the quarters would be dragged through the streets of London and displayed on stakes in prominent places, most often London Bridge. The dignified public of London would stroll across the bridge to see the heads of the latest criminals that had been executed. Often they would be left there until the birds had picked the skulls clean."

"Gruesome," said Simon.

"Sweet," said Nish.

"Sickening," said Sam.

"Awesome," said Nish.

"I want outta here," said Lars.

"I wanna *be* here!" said Nish. "My very own display – 'Wayne Nishikawa – the World's Most Twisted and Evil Hockey Player'!"

THE SCREECH OWLS HAD COME TO LONDON THE morning after Hallowe'en. They had left their homes in Tamarack, where the trees were bare and a light snow had fallen during the afternoon, and had flown through the night to London to find themselves landing on an exquisitely sunny day in England, the rolling fields below them seemingly as brown and soft as rabbit fur as the plane approached Gatwick.

It had been a quiet flight, apart from the initial ruckus caused by Nish as he tried to board with three carry-on bags: his packsack, holding mostly comic books and a portable CD player, and two bags of trick-or-treat loot. But after his Hallowe'en candy had been stashed with the rest of the luggage, much to his regret, the flight had been smooth and uneventful, the team members sound asleep along four rows and Muck quietly reading a massive history of London in a seat next to Mr. Dillinger.

It was one of the farthest "road" trips the Owls had ever undertaken, but already the least expensive. It would probably cost more, Travis thought to himself, to drive the hour or so over to the next town and play a league match than it was to fly to London for a week of competition.

The trip had been Data's idea. He had read about a special promotion in *The Hockey News*. A new, British-based sports-equipment company, International In-Line, was seeking to break into the North American market with their in-line skates, and to gain some publicity they were holding a contest open to peewee-level teams. The winners would travel to London to play in an exhibition tournament against the Wembley Young Lions, a British team of twelve- and thirteen-year-olds that was said to be the best in-line team in all of Europe.

Data said the Screech Owls should enter.

"We don't even *play* in-line!" argued Dmitri Yakushev, Travis's linemate.

"What's the difference?" said Simon Milliken. "We play *hockey* — it's the same game whether you're on blades or wheels, as far as I can see.

"*I'm* on wheels," Data joked, spinning his wheelchair, "and I still consider myself a hockey player."

Slowly, the Owls warmed to Data's suggestion. Travis, Dmitri, and Sarah, the Owls' first line, often used in-line skates in the summer, particularly when there was roadwork being done around Tamarack and they could find smooth new pavement to skate on. Dmitri had proved to be as fast on wheels as he was on skates. A few times, the Owls had even put together in-line shinny matches down at the tennis courts when no one else was using them. But they had never played as a team, and certainly never against a real in-line team.

They had never even heard of such a thing.

Fahd Noorizadeh agreed with Data. "We're a hockey team. We all have in-line skates. So now we're also an in-line team, okay?"

To enter, each team had to state, in fifty words or less, why they should be chosen. The manufacturer would choose the best dozen entries, and the winner would then be selected by a draw.

It had been Fahd's idea to stuff the ballot box. There was no limit to the number of times you could enter, so the Owls, several of whom subscribed to the hockey magazine, cut out their entry forms and Derek got his father, Mr. Dillinger, to photocopy hundreds more down at his office for them to fill out.

Travis never expected anything to come of it all. He had dutifully filled out several forms, always stumbling over the fifty-word reason. "The Screech Owls are a fun team of good athletes, and we would all enjoy a trip to London . . . ," he wrote, and "The Screech Owls are one of the best peewee hockey teams in North America, and we would like to prove ourselves internationally. . . ." It wasn't great, but he'd done as asked and mailed them off.

A month later the Owls were notified that the team was a finalist in the competition.

The entry they selected had come from Sarah.

"There would be no Screech Owls hockey team if not for Muck Munro, our coach," Sarah had written, "and since the only thing Muck loves as much as hockey is history, this trip to historical London would be one way for us to show our appreciation for the greatest coach ever."

"That's only forty-eight words," Nish had said, shaking his head after he had counted out loud. "You're still two short."

"Would '*without Nish*' help?" Sam Bennett had asked.

Two more weeks passed and the draw took place, with a phone call from London, England, to Sarah to say her entry had been drawn.

The Screech Owls were headed for London.

International In-Line would cover all costs: the flight, accommodation, food, transportation within London, and entry to various attractions – including Madame Tussaud's famous wax museum and the Chamber of Horrors.

The Owls now had only two problems to overcome.

First, they needed to convince coach Muck Munro it was a good idea.

And second, they had to become an in-line hockey team.

3

TALKING MUCK MUNRO INTO TAKING THE
Screech Owls to a foreign country to play a sport
he had barely heard of turned out to be less
difficult than they anticipated.

The reason was Mr. Dillinger, who had been
an early convert to the idea of the trip. The Owls'
balding, roly-poly manager had loved the idea
from the moment he heard about Data's and
Fahd's wild plan to stuff the ballot box, and he
had moved quickly to get the parents behind the
scheme. The trip would be cheap, would last only
a week, and he would personally ensure that no
one fell behind on their school work. It would,
after all, also be an educational trip, a once-in-a-
lifetime opportunity to see one of the world's
great cities.

Mr. Dillinger had used cost as the way to convince the parents.

For Muck, he used the past.

Muck loved hockey, but he adored history,
especially military history. He knew all the
American Civil War battlefields, and had walked
the Plains of Abraham in Quebec City, where

the most significant battle in Canada's history had taken place. But his great passion was British history: Nelson at the Battle of Trafalgar, Wellington taking on Napoleon at Waterloo, Churchill's inspirational speeches to the Allies during the worst days of the Second World War . . .

Mr. Dillinger caught Muck after a practice in early fall, not long after the ice had gone in at the Tamarack rink. He had come armed with brochures. Trafalgar Square . . . the great statue of Wellington . . . the British War Museum . . . the Victoria and Albert Museum . . . the Churchill display at Madame Tussaud's . . . the Tower of London . . .

"I don't know anything about this in-line ridiculousness," Muck had protested.

"Muck," Mr. Dillinger had said in his jolliest voice, "there's a net at both ends, there are boards all around, there are hockey sticks, and if you score a goal it counts as *one*. What's to know?"

"But hockey's played on ice. Ice you can skate on."

"They *will* be skating. Every one of them already knows how to in-line skate, and the manufacturer's providing all the latest equipment. You can wear your same old clothes to coach in, for heaven's sake."

Muck had looked up, one eyebrow cocked higher than the other. "What about skates? I'm not putting on any in-line skates."

"You won't have to," Mr. Dillinger said. "Wear sneakers, just like you do in lacrosse. I promise you, you won't have to wear skates with wheels."

"*Training* wheels," Muck sneered.

But he was clearly weakening, and Mr. Dillinger took his opening.

"Wellington's monument . . . ," he said in almost a singsongy voice, "Nelson's Column in Trafalgar Square . . . Downing Street . . ."

Muck raised his eyebrow even higher. "I won't have to put on those silly skates?"

"I promise."

"We better call a practice."

The Owls practised at the high school's double gymnasium, which was almost the size of a regulation in-line rink, though it lacked the curved corners that a rink would have.

Travis had a hard time adjusting to in-line hockey. His game, on ice, was working the corners and quick stops and starts. To stop with in-line skates, he had to press down on the brake, and it took a conscious effort.

The skating was fine on open ice – or, perhaps open *floor* would be more apt.

Dmitri took to the game as if he'd been playing on wheels all his life. The sleek Russian seemed twice as fast as anyone else, with the possible exception of Sarah, and he could also stickhandle better than anyone at top speed.

The stickhandling took some getting used to. They played with a plastic object that was a bit like a puck, a bit like a flattened ball. The Owls, of course, were used to regular pucks, but every one of them had spent so much time playing ball hockey on the street and in their driveways that they adapted easily to the new object. The hard part was putting the skating together with the "puck" handling.

Travis eventually got to like skating on wheels. He missed the sense of the blades cutting into fresh ice, but the feel was smooth and quick, and he found that with practice his turns got faster, though never quite as fast as when he was on ice skates.

The equipment was different, lighter, less bulky, but still it was obviously hockey equipment. All the Owls liked experimenting with the new game, and there were different offside rules and no blueline, which Nish claimed to adore.

When they boarded the flight bound for Gatwick International Airport, they had yet to play a single in-line game, but they knew their positions, had a number of plays worked out on Muck's blackboard, and they thought they were ready.

Ready to prove themselves the best in-line hockey team in all of London, anyway.

4

TRAVIS WOKE UP IN THE FIRST-AID ROOM OF Madame Tussaud's. Mr. Dillinger and Sarah Cuthbertson, who had also felt like fainting, had stayed with him while the rest of the Owls continued their tour.

Travis felt like he was rising out of a bad dream. At first he thought he was home in Tamarack and his father was shaking him awake. When he opened his eyes he was surprised to see Mr. Dillinger's big moustache bouncing in a smile, but almost immediately he remembered he was in London and they were on a tour.

"What happened?" he asked, blinking.

"You fainted."

"So did I, a bit," added Sarah. She was sitting up, fixing her light brown hair into a ponytail with an elastic. Her bangs looked damp with perspiration, though the room was cool.

Travis shuddered, fearing the obvious. "No one else?" he asked.

Mr. Dillinger shook his head, his eyes closed in sympathy.

"They're gonna kill me," Travis said, wincing.

He did not mean "they." He meant Wayne Nishikawa, his best friend in the world, but also his worst enemy in the world when it came to being singled out and humiliated. Nish would never let him live it down.

"People faint here all the time," said Mr. Dillinger. "Happens once a week or so. The tour guide also told us that attempts have been made by people to stay alone in the Chamber of Horrors, but no one has ever got through the night."

Travis nodded. He felt better. He sat up, his head swimming a bit, but it cleared as he stayed there, resting.

Travis smiled at Sarah. "You okay?"

Sarah smiled back. "I'm fine." She looked a little pale.

"We'll meet the rest of them outside," said Mr. Dillinger. "Muck has a little surprise in store for everyone."

"No blood and guts?" asked Travis.

"No blood and guts," smiled Mr. Dillinger.

"Remember," Muck said, standing in front of his assembled team, "it's only a practice – it doesn't count."

And yet it did count.

International In-Line had organized a quick "refreshment" match against the Young Lions of

Wembley, the team that the Owls would later be playing in the official game before a big crowd at historic Wembley Stadium. No one, however, would be invited to watch this game. It would be held on a temporary surface set up on a grassy field near the Serpentine, the shallow artificial lake on the edge of Hyde Park, not far from Marble Arch and Edgware Road, where the Owls had been put up in a pleasant hotel just off the main thoroughfare.

It would count in the Owls' minds because – unbeknownst to the organizers – it would be the very first in-line game this team from Canada had ever played.

They walked from the hotel down Edgware Road in silence, each Owl deep in his or her own thoughts. Fahd and Jesse Highboy took turns walking with Data as he guided his electric wheelchair over the paths and grass. Muck and Mr. Dillinger walked ahead, Muck fascinated by the little shops with their dozens of just-off-the-press newspapers shouting out the latest world events, Mr. Dillinger fascinated by the number of Middle Eastern cafés with men and women sitting inside, sipping coffee and smoking water pipes.

Travis was overwhelmed with the bustle, the life, the energy of the street. He marvelled at the cars roaring down the "wrong" side of the street, listened in amazement to the dozens of different languages, and giggled when he turned the corner by Marble Arch and saw Nish, up ahead, scrambling out of a McDonald's with a Big Mac in his hand. A little snack before the game.

They walked over the green grass and under towering elm trees down toward the Serpentine, where people were strolling about the path, feeding the ducks and geese. There were paddle-boats out on the water and, on the far side, a grey-haired man in a wetsuit was swimming laps opposite a little restaurant.

It was a lovely day, the sun shining and a light breeze plucking the odd dead leaf from the trees and sending it spinning down. There were so few leaves on the ground, however, that Travis won-dered if they had sweepers hiding behind the big trunks waiting for one to land so they could race out and be off with it before anyone noticed. He had never seen such a beautifully kept park.

The playing surface had been laid out behind the park office. It looked to Travis like a typical Canadian outdoor rink before the first snow, but as the Owls drew closer they saw it was brand new and that the blue playing surface was made up of hard plastic panels. There were nets at both ends and a line across centre, the only line on the rink.

The Young Lions were already warming up, and the Owls were already intimidated.

The young Brits seemed to skate effortlessly. None was as quick as Dmitri, but all were smooth and seemed to cut and stop as easily on this surface as any Owl could on the fresh ice of Tamarack. They seemed much bigger than the Owls, too, though it may have been partly the extra height that came from being on skates while the Owls, standing around the boards watching, were all wearing sneakers.

"They're *good*," said Fahd.

"They're nuttin'," said Nish.

"They're good," confirmed Muck. "We'll have our hands full – and more."

There was a tent set up for the Owls to dress. Muck and Mr. Dillinger were met by a balding, red-faced man with bad teeth, who waved the team inside.

"My name is Mr. Wolfe," the man said in a clipped, uppity accent once the Owls were all sitting around their dressing room. "But we needn't stand on formality here – you're welcome to call me 'Sir.'"

Only Mr. Dillinger, out of politeness, and Fahd, out of being Fahd, laughed at the man's silly joke. Travis did not care for older men who acted as if everything they said was funny and that they, and they alone, would decide what was humorous or not. Travis could tell by the way Mr. Wolfe glanced so eagerly around, his upper lip dancing over dark and decayed teeth, that he was anxious to establish himself as the only funny person in the room.

"Ahem," Mr. Wolfe coughed uneasily when he realized he might no longer have their full attention. "First of all, I'd like to welcome you all to London, England, site of the world's first International In-Line Peewee Championship."

Travis stared down at his skates. He was embarrassed by talk like this. Mr. Wolfe – who spat slightly as he spoke – was acting like this was a major event, not an exhibition match, in a sport that really didn't count for much, with one team from a country not known for hockey against a team that had never played a single game before.

"We're deeply honoured to play host to the Canadian Barn Owls," said Mr. Wolfe.

"Screech," Sam corrected.

"Beg your pardon?"

"*Screech* Owls – we're the Screech Owls."

"Yes," Mr. Wolfe said in an explosion of spittle. "Well, yes, of course. Screech Owls. Pardon me. This will be a pivotal moment in the history of Canadian–British relations . . ."

Travis shook his head as the man prattled on. He tuned Mr. Wolfe out, and didn't hear another word of the long-winded and silly speech. Instead, he turned his mind to "visioning" his game.

Travis liked to do this before a big ice hockey match. Sometimes he could almost put himself into a trance imagining the game coming up.

Only there was one problem: *How do you envision a game you have never played?*

5

TRAVIS SOON FOUND OUT.

The Screech Owls played in-line hockey as if they were indeed the Barn Owls from Canada. Everything seemed to go wrong from the very start. First, Travis forgot to kiss his sweater as he pulled it over his head, and Mr. Dillinger hadn't found time to sew the "C" for captain onto the new jersey supplied by the manufacturer. Then Travis slipped in the warm-up and went down hard on one knee. He failed to hit the crossbar on his warm-up shots, finding the plastic ball the manufacturer wanted them to use flew off the end of his new stick quite unlike a vulcanized rubber puck shot off a real hockey stick. He was high and to the right with everything. His shots seemed to hook the way a golf ball will suddenly seem to turn in mid-air and head off in an unintended direction.

Then they dropped the ball – and matters got worse.

Sarah's line, as always, took the first shift. Dmitri was on right, ready for the quick break; Travis was on left, ready to fall back if Sarah lost the faceoff; Fahd and Nish were ready on defence; Jeremy was in goal.

But the referee threw down the ball instead of just dropping it. Not only was Sarah unable to pluck it out of the air, but it bounced wildly. The Young Lions centre scooped it out of the air on the second bounce, flicking it off to a winger who had already burst inside and past Fahd.

Travis first thought it was offside, but when no whistle blew he remembered that the rules for in-line were quite different. The only line was at centre, meaning players had to cross centre before dumping it in, but no bluelines meant there was nothing to stop a winger from floating on the other side of the play and trusting to cherry-pick a long pass for a goal.

That was exactly what happened. The player behind Fahd clipped the ball down with his glove and slapped a hard shot at Jeremy as soon as it struck the playing surface.

Jeremy managed to block the shot with his chest, but it bounced straight up in the air as he went down, and the winger merely skated in and bunted the floating object out of the air and into the net.

Young Lions 1, Screech Owls 0.

"Cherry-picker," Nish said as he brushed by the scorer, elbowing him slightly as he passed.

"Wha's tha', mate?" a decidedly non-hockey voice asked.

Nish answered by slashing the player across his shin pads. The whistle blew and Nish was headed for the penalty box. Thirty seconds later he was back out, the Young Lions having gone ahead 2–0.

Muck ordered Sarah's line off in favour of Andy Higgins's line.

"This is impossible!" Sarah said as she slumped on the bench.

"We've never played this game before," Travis said between gulps of breath. "We just have to be patient."

"If we wait too long," Dmitri gasped, "they'll be ahead 100–0."

The Young Lions scored again on a fast-break play, and then on a deflection, and went to 5–0 on a pretty give-and-go between their best player, a lanky kid with long blond hair flowing out the back of his helmet, and their top defenceman.

"*We're getting creamed!*" Sam said, throwing down her stick angrily as she came off the court.

Muck turned to her. "Pick up your stick and go to the dressing room."

Sam stared back, startled, but she knew better than to argue. She also knew what Muck was doing. They were guests. They were representing their country. This was neither the time nor the place for poor sportsmanship. In Muck's view, there was never a time or a place.

Sam looped off her helmet, her red hair a

wet tangle, and dragged herself off, Mr. Dillinger hurrying after her.

"We can't afford to lose her," said Derek.

"We can't afford to quit, either," said Travis. "We've got to get our act together."

Slowly, ever so slowly, the Owls began to find their game. It was not as polished as that of the Young Lions, not as pretty to watch, and certainly not as effective, but little by little they began turning back the Young Lions' rushes and mounting a few of their own.

Travis could feel the game coming to him. He always knew he was playing his best ice hockey when he forgot about skating, when his skates became as comfortable as slippers. He was still acutely aware now of the effort he was making, but there was no pain in his insteps and, several times he almost forgot he was on wheels instead of blades.

Dmitri and Sarah, too, were coming around. Sarah made a beautiful rush up centre, chased by the Lion with the thick flow of blond hair, and flipped a pass, high over the shoulder of the opposing defence, to Dmitri, coming in fast on the right side.

Dmitri tried his trademark move, the shoulder deke followed by a roofed shot to the water bottle, but the strange plastic ball seemed to squirt off the end of his backhand and ticked harmlessly off the post.

No matter — at least they had *hit* a post!

Nish was settling down as well. He was using his strength to work the corners, and it became increasingly obvious the Young Lions were shying away from going into corners with the big Owls defenceman. Nish was hitting hard, and often, and it struck Travis that perhaps their opponents were not used to the body contact of ice hockey.

Nish levelled the blond centre behind the Owls' net and came up with the ball, settling it on the end of his stick with a quick little pat.

Nish looked up ice — or up *plastic* — and eyed Travis, who broke hard across the surface for a pass.

Nish hit him perfectly, the ball looping over the sticks of two checkers and landing, perfectly, on Travis's blade.

He had barely corralled it when he flicked a quick backhand through a defenceman's legs to a spot where Sarah was headed.

Sarah caught the ball in her skates, dragged the ball-bearing wheels just long enough to kick it up onto her stick, and broke hard down the left side. Nish steamrolled straight up centre to join the rush, and Dmitri was already far down the right side.

With only one defender back, the Young Lions had no idea what to do. The defenceman backpedalled and fell as Sarah burst around him. Sarah had the shot, Dmitri flying in for the rebound. But instead of shooting, Sarah did a beautiful back pass to Nish, who was already swinging with all his strength.

Nish's stick clipped the ball oddly, almost like a foul in baseball. From Travis's angle, he could see perfectly what happened next.

The ball shot off Nish's stick, heading wide of the net – only to slice sharply back and all but curl right around the goalie into the net.

Young Lions 5, Screech Owls 1.

The Owls' bench burst into cheers, as if Nish had scored the winning goal in the Stanley Cup. They ignored the referee's whistle and poured over the boards. Even Mr. Dillinger, with a big white towel wrapped around his neck, was dancing and war-whooping across the playing surface and then snapping his towel at imaginary enemies.

Nish was at the bottom of the heap, screaming that he was going to die, but no one paid him the slightest heed.

When Travis got to him, Nish had a grin bigger than the Hallowe'en pumpkin that Travis's mother had lit with a candle and set in the front window. Nish seemed even to burn with his own inner candle.

"Your shot sliced!" Travis shouted at him.

"Eh?"

"Your shot curved right around the goalie!"

"Of course it did. You think I don't know what I'm doing?"

Travis was laughing too hard to care what

Nish was saying. The Owls had scored their first-ever goal as an in-line hockey team, and it had been a beauty.

It would, however, be their last for this day. After the Owls had cleared the court, the Young Lions scored three more goals to end the game 8-1.

Travis was glad it was over. He had seen a dozen areas where the Owls could improve, and Muck had surely seen a dozen more. Data was already typing notes to himself on his laptop. The Owls would improve.

The two teams lined up to shake hands, and Mr. Wolfe moved to the centre of the playing surface with a microphone in his hand. When he spoke, speakers at the far end crackled and echoed, but it was impossible to make out anything he was saying, so he gave up and simply stood at centre and shouted.

"Thank you, teams, for this early demonstration of what will truly be a magnificent exhibition match at Wembley Stadium next Tuesday evening." He paused, casting a critical eye over the lined-up Screech Owls, barely able to hide his disappointment at the level of play. "We know the Snow Owls are tired from their long trip . . ."

"*Screech* Owls!" shouted Sarah, fire dancing in her eyes.

"Yes, Screech Owls. We know they will recover and the big game will be more competitive. We would like to honour the most valuable players from each side, however, with a special gift to each."

An assistant ran out with two boxes, the tops loosened, and began to open them up.

"Would Edward Rose from the Young Lions step forward, please?" Mr. Wolfe asked.

The blond centre took his helmet off and shook his hair. Even when wet it seemed to shine like sunlight.

"Ohhhhhh," said Sam.

"Yes!" agreed Sarah, giggling.

"Pathetic," said Nish.

The assistant pulled a golden helmet out of a box and handed it to Mr. Wolfe.

"In England," Mr. Wolfe said grandly, "we say you have won a cap when you play for your country. In some European hockey leagues, the leading scorer for each team wears a golden helmet."

"We did that in Sweden," Lars said to Travis.

"We are hoping to bring that tradition to international in-line competition," Mr. Wolfe continued, "to cap our young stars with a golden helmet. These are prototypes, children, and not yet ready for competition, but we thought they would make a wonderful souvenir for the teams. Congratulations, Mr. Rose."

As Mr. Wolfe and Edward Rose shook hands and posed for a photograph, the two teams rapped their sticks on the playing surface.

It seemed a bit much to Travis — acting as if a little practice game meant anything — but he thought the helmets were a neat idea, if somewhat silly. Why, he had often wondered, would any team want their most dangerous man on the ice identified at all times? Or most dangerous *woman*, for Sarah was usually the Owls' leading scorer.

"And," Mr. Wolfe continued, "for the Hoot Owls —"

"*Screech* Owls!" Sam shouted angrily.

"Hmmm? Ah, yes, for the Screech Owls, the MVP for today is Mr. Wayne . . . Nishi . . . Nisha . . ."

"Nishikawa!" Nish shouted out, skating over to receive his prize.

"Yes, of course. Nish-i-kawa," Mr. Wolfe said, spittle flying in every direction. "Congratulations to you, young man."

Nish took the helmet, bowed gracefully in the direction of each team, and sticks began rapping on the playing surface to honour him.

But not all the sticks, Travis noticed. Many of the Young Lions, including Edward Rose, the star player, were refusing to salute the Screech Owl who had knocked them about in the corners before scoring a grandstand goal.

This, Travis told himself, was going to get awfully interesting.

6

MUCK WAS BLOCKING THE DRESSING-ROOM door when they headed off the playing surface. He had his arms folded over his chest but didn't look particularly angry with any of them.

"Walk it off," he told them. "Cool down slowly, otherwise you'll tighten up so bad you won't be able to play next game . . ." Muck smiled, almost to himself: ". . . not that anyone actually *played* this one, of course."

The Owls got the message. It wasn't so much about cooling down as it was about thinking about the game. Muck knew if they got into the dressing room, their thoughts would quickly turn to London and the sights, but before the inevitable happened he wanted them to think about what went wrong in the game and what, if anything, each of them might do to correct matters.

Travis kicked off his skates and headed out, barefoot, along the path heading for the Serpentine. The pebbles bothered his feet, so he switched over to the grass, walking toward the trees and some welcome shade.

Travis thought about all he'd done wrong: forgetting to kiss his sweater, not adapting well to the newfangled "puck," failing to understand the new rules . . . He was replaying the disastrous game in his head when he heard a familiar voice.

"Yes, Fox here . . ."

There was a mammoth elm between Travis and the voice, but he knew it instantly: Mr. Wolfe.

"Fox here," the man was saying rather breathlessly into his cellphone. "That you, Parley?"

Mr. Wolfe seemed to be having trouble with his connection, repeating again and again his question, finally almost barking it out.

Travis started giggling. What was wrong with this strange man and his memory? He'd called the Screech Owls the Barn Owls. He'd called them the Snow Owls. He'd called them the Hoot Owls.

And now Mr. Wolfe couldn't even keep his own name straight: "*Fox* here," he'd said.

Travis shook his head. Maybe it was just a nickname.

Perhaps Mr. Wolfe was just one of those legendary British eccentrics Muck and Mr. Dillinger had been laughing about on the flight over – a man so absent-minded he couldn't remember his *own* name, let alone the names of those he'd just met.

"Yes . . . yes . . . yes." Mr. Wolfe's voice was fading as he walked deeper into the trees, still speaking into the phone. "They have the helmets – it went fine."

Travis smiled. Perhaps he was absent-minded and mixed up, but at least he was thorough. It was hard to fault him for that.

By the end of the trip he might even remember that they were the Screech Owls.

Travis shook off the distraction and went back to thinking about what he himself could do to turn the fortunes of the Owls around. He could check harder. He could play smarter. He could try harder. He *would* try harder.

Sam had obviously been unable to shake it off. When Travis and the others returned from their thinking walk, she was already sitting in a far corner of the dressing room, her face red and sad as she took the tape off her shin pads and worked it onto her beloved tape ball.

She had been assembling her famous ball for nearly a year now. She had started it without really noticing, ripping off her stretchy plastic shin-pad tape and, instead of tossing it in the garbage can, rolling it together into a little ball. Over time, it grew and grew. Sarah started adding her equipment tape to the ball, then Travis offered his, and now most of the Owls were routinely ripping off their tape and carrying it over to Sam to add to the collection, which was now roughly the size of a soccer ball.

There was only one player who routinely refused. Nish thought the tape ball was "stupid" and "girlish." He would say things like "Do you think Paul Kariya keeps a tape ball?" Several times he tried to hide it on Sam.

But there was no fooling around this time, not even from Nish. Travis thought his friend was about to burst, so proud was he of his new golden helmet, but even Nish sometimes had the good sense to keep quiet. Especially after an 8–1 loss. And especially after Muck had taken the unusual step of sending one of the players to the dressing room for bad behaviour.

The silence was unbearable, but it could be broken by only one person: Muck.

And Muck would do it in his own inimitable way.

Travis undressed slowly, his legs burning and his feet cramping with pain. It always puzzled him how you could be in good shape from sports and yet, with each new season, each new activity, feel as if you had done nothing but sit in a lawn chair from the moment the last season ended. It happened in the first week of hockey, and the first few practices in lacrosse. It happened when he went skiing for the first time each winter. It happened when he broke out his mountain bike each spring, and again when they started playing touch football at school in the fall. And now it was happening after his first-ever game of in-line hockey.

It was, he thought to himself, as if every activity had its own unique muscles in addition to all the others, and it was these special hidden ones that hurt with each new sport.

Mr. Dillinger was picking up the jerseys and stuffing them into a duffle bag for washing when Muck, dressed as always in his old sweatpants and raggedy windbreaker, came in and stopped dead in the centre of the room.

The coach had his reading glasses on. He stared hard over them toward the far corner, where Sam, who had stopped moulding her tape ball for the moment, mouthed the word "sorry" in his direction.

Muck made no response. He stared a moment longer, then looked down at his clipboard.

Strange, Travis thought – there was not a word written on it. And yet anyone who knew anything about the game of hockey, in any of its forms, could have written volumes about what the Owls had done wrong in this game.

Perhaps Muck had decided, instead, to write down everything they had done right.

Muck plucked off his reading glasses and stuffed them, unprotected, into his windbreaker pocket. "Be in the lobby at one o'clock sharp," he said.

Fahd asked the obvious question. "What for?"

"We're headed first for Westminster Abbey and then the Tower of London."

Muck turned back toward Sam, still sitting sheepishly in the corner.

"We have a player to lock up."

Travis felt much better. He had showered and changed and was waiting in the hotel lobby by 12:45 with most of the rest of the Owls. He'd left Nish in their room, sitting like he was hypnotized in front of the big mirror over the dresser.

The moment they got back, Nish had put on the golden helmet, and he hadn't taken it off since. Travis eventually concluded Nish would have showered with it on if he had to, but Nish showered so rarely this was not really very likely. Nish declared himself ready after a few more checks in the mirror, but Travis had given up waiting and gone down ahead of his roommates.

Sarah and Sam were already sitting on the wide sofa in the lobby, both of them talking about the blond kid, Edward Rose, who had starred for the Young Lions. Travis talked a while with Data and Fahd, who were trying to figure out if they could use Fahd's cellphone to transfer digital photographs from Data's camera to his laptop – the sort of technical talk that put Travis fast asleep if it went on too long.

Finally, all were ready to go – even Nish, despite the fact that his sweaty hair had taken on the shape of the helmet he'd been so reluctant to remove – and the Owls headed up the Edgware Road to the nearest Tube station, where they caught the Yellow Line, which would carry them straight through to the Westminster stop.

Travis was fascinated by the Underground. He liked the ticketing machines. He loved the sense that he was headed so deep into the ground he might have been descending into a coal mine. The Owls went down, down, down seemingly endless escalators, past billboards advertising products he had never heard of before.

The Tube itself was thrilling. The doors slid open, the Owls piled on, whistles blew, the doors shut like gentle sideways guillotines, and the train jerked and started off, almost immediately grinding and screeching as it headed into a long turn before the next stop in the line.

"Paddington Station!" Sam and Sarah screamed out at once.

"Let's switch to platform 9¾!" shouted Simon, laughing.

"What's *he* talking about?" Nish growled in Travis's ear.

"Platform 9¾ . . . ," Travis explained with a slight look of disbelief at his friend. ". . . Paddington Station . . . the Harry Potter books . . . you know."

"I don't read books," Nish grinned slyly, "*remember?*"

35

On and on the train rattled and shook, screeching to a halt every so often, jerking to a start again. The girls kept calling out the name of each station — "Notting Hill Gate!" "Kensington!" "Victoria Station!" "St. James's Park!" — and Travis, with his eyes closed, imagined how much his grandmother would enjoy this. She was forever reading English mysteries, forever talking about Agatha Christie and Miss Marple and pushing them on Travis when he was up at the cottage. She would have loved this. It was like travelling through the pages of one of her books.

The train reached Westminster and they all piled out just as Big Ben struck the half-hour. The sun was shining down warm and bright — an unlikely day to have back in Canada for November, Travis thought. They seemed to have come up out of the Underground into the height of summer holidays: crowds everywhere, tourists with cameras, uniformed schoolchildren being led by tight-lipped, back-ward-walking teachers shouting at stragglers, older people wearing colourful arm bands to identify them for their tour guides, dark-suited businessmen looking as if they wished they could stab their way through the crowds with their umbrellas, and street vendors hawking everything from miniature Big Bens to bobbies' helmets and ice cream.

Nish already had a cone in each hand by the time Travis reached the top of the stairs and stepped out, blinking, into the sunshine.

"*Stereo!*" Nish shouted, and raised both treats to his mouth so he could lick them at the same time.

Mr. Dillinger had his big guidebook out and pointed to the various sights: Big Ben and the Houses of Parliament, the giant London Eye ferris wheel turning high on the other side of the Thames, the beginnings of still-green St. James's Park, Whitehall – where, Muck jumped in, "Churchill ran the War Room" – and, of course, Westminster Abbey, with its manicured lawns and high grey stone steeples.

Muck and Mr. Dillinger let the Owls enjoy their treats, then led the team on a tour of the Abbey with a young priest who said he had relatives in Halifax and wondered if perhaps any of the players knew them.

He told them, in far too much detail, the history of the church, how there had been churches on this site since the eighth century, though the present building had been started in 1050 by Edward the Confessor.

"Last person in the world I'd hang around with," whispered Nish in that strange voice of his that carried like a shout. All the Owls giggled, Nish blushed, and Muck gave him a sharp look while the tour carried on.

Travis had never seen such a celebration of death. Back home there were cemeteries, but no one in Tamarack had anything like some of the monuments on display in the Abbey. Nor did anyone in Canada, as far as he knew, get buried in the floor and covered with a massive slab of stone, with a brass plate over it telling visitors who, exactly, they were walking over.

They were shown the graves – or tombs, as the priest called them – of a dozen or more kings and queens.

"Why's everyone named Henry?" Nish whispered loudly at one point. "Couldn't they think of any other names?"

Muck shot him another look, but Nish was on a roll.

He suggested that the choir practising in the main part of the Abbey could do with an electric guitar and drums. He pretended to gag when they were shown through Poet's Corner. He thought the wooden Coronation Chair – "Made in 1300," the young priest said, "and every monarch since has been crowned on it" – looked like an outhouse seat waiting for the hole to be cut in it.

"Where to now?" asked the kindly young priest after he had shown them all there was to see.

"The Tower of London," said Muck. "I now have *two* players I need to lock up for a while."

7

THEY CAUGHT THE GREEN LINE, AND IN A FEW short minutes were at the Tower Hill stop and coming onto a perfect view of famous Tower Bridge, where Data and Fahd insisted on lining everyone up for a team photograph.

Travis had never imagined a place at once so lovely and so terrifying. The Tower of London took your breath away with its beauty, and took it away again with its history.

It was a kaleidoscope of colour. Exquisite gardens, perfect lawns, different-coloured towers, and wardens dressed exactly like the picture on the front of the gin bottle Travis's grandmother liked to get out when she was settling down with a good mystery novel. They even had the same name: beefeater.

Travis thought the beefeaters' strange costumes fit perfectly with the stories the guides told them as they moved about. Bright red uniforms, bright red history – red with blood.

Everywhere they looked, every word they heard, seemed to have blood in it somewhere. Even the birds.

Travis had noticed the ravens at the Tower as soon as the Screech Owls arrived at the front gates, and he had recognized them immediately, thanks to his grandfather's obsession with birdwatching. He had told Travis astonishing stories about the large black birds.

According to Travis's grandfather, ravens lived almost as long as people. They could "talk" and could imitate dozens of animals. Inuit hunters said they guided them to caribou and seal, showing the hunters where the game might be hiding in the hope that, in return, they would get small portions of the kill.

But none of old Mr. Lindsay's chatter about his favourite birds compared to what the beefeater wardens told the Owls.

The ravens at the Tower of London were famous. "In certain parts of the world," the guide told them, "ravens are held to be bad luck, foretellers of death. Ravens were well known for following troops into battle, where they would then pick the dead down to their bones. There are parts of England still where a man will tip his hat to a raven if one flies by, just as he would if it were a hearse passing on the road. But here they are said to be the greatest of luck."

"Luck?" asked Fahd. "How's that?"

"They're our lucky charm," the guide said, smiling. "We take the greatest care of them. Every single day, for example, I will feed them exactly six ounces of raw bloody meat – as the king once decreed. We also give them special biscuits that have been soaked in blood for treats."

"Why?" asked Liz.

"We want to keep them here and keep them content," the guide said, then winked. "Mind you, we clip their wings, too, so it's not as if they're going to fly far away. But they have left in the past. We had one who didn't like it here and took up at a local pub for a few years. His name was Grog. I suspect he had a drinking problem."

"Are you *serious*?" asked Fahd.

"No. Are you?"

"Always!" sighed Sam.

"Well, young man, I'm being serious, too. We have seven ravens here at the moment. They all have names. That's Hardey hopping across the lawn over there." He pointed to a bird jumping toward a group of tourists. "He's easily the most famous of our Tower ravens – and an ill-tempered lot he is, too. Don't point a finger at him or he'll snap it off.

"There's Gomer and Thor and Cedric over there. And Hugine, that's a female. The others are about. Just keep your eyes out and your fingers in."

"Why do you keep them?" Jeremy asked.

"It was always said that if the ravens ever left the Tower, the Crown would fall. That's why

Charles II decreed more than three hundred years ago that there must always be at least six ravens here. And that's why we always make sure there is an extra, usually two, just in case.

"If the ravens ever leave the Tower, I'm right behind them — let me tell you that."

The beefeater spoke with a bit of a chuckle and a wink, but Travis could not help but get the feeling that the man truly believed the legend.

Still, it seemed ludicrous. How could there possibly be any connection between the ravens of the Tower of London and the survival of the British Crown.

Mr. Dillinger had told them that the Crown Jewels were held at the Tower of London, and this, Travis had presumed, would be the main attraction for tourists. The Owls had apparently come at a lucky time, for there would be a royal procession later in the week, with various members of the royal family — "*Prince William!*" Sarah had shrieked, "*Prince Harry!*" Sam had squealed — parading to the Tower of London to celebrate the seven hundredth anniversary of the Crown Jewels being held at the Tower.

The jewels were spectacular, but they paled considerably when held up against the history. On Tower Hill, just outside the window, the beefeater told them, more than three hundred people, many of them famous historical figures, were executed.

Inside the tower, they were imprisoned and tortured, often with the hideous thumbscrew, which tightened down on a prisoner's thumbnail until he was willing to confess to any crime at all if only the torturers would stop.

There was even a ancient axe with a huge blade, which, the guide said, had been used to behead Anne Boleyn, the first of Henry VIII's two wives to be executed at the Tower. Here, too, was where Sir Walter Raleigh, once the greatest hero in all of England, was imprisoned for thirteen years for supposedly plotting against the King. Raleigh was later beheaded at Westminster Abbey, but, the guide said, "Sir Walter's ghost is said still to walk at night in what they once called the Garden Tower but has long been known as the Bloody Tower."

The most moving story of all concerned the Princes in the Tower. Edward V was to be the young king of the country, but his evil uncle, Richard III, took Edward and his younger brother, locked them up in the Bloody Tower, and took the crown for himself.

The princes were never seen again.

"Edward V was twelve years old," the beefeater told the Owls, "his brother only ten."

Travis heard a sharp intake of breath behind him. It was Sam.

Edward would have been exactly the same age as the Owls.

"As legend has it," the beefeater continued, his smooth voice dropping low, "the older boy was stabbed with a dagger and the younger suffocated with a pillow. Their bodies were not found until nearly two hundred years later, when a priest was searching beneath the stairs you see over there and uncovered an old chest that had been buried beneath stones. He pulled it out and opened it up and found two small skeletons inside, still in their sleeping clothes."

Travis heard a quick sob from behind. Sam again. Then a choke.

Sarah.

"What did they look like?" Fahd asked.

Travis winced. Fahd always asked the most ridiculous questions.

"Just bones," said the beefeater. "Bones and a bit of cloth."

"No," Fahd said. "The princes – what did they look like when they were alive?"

"Ahhhhhh," the guide said, nodding. "Well, we don't really know all that much about them, young man. They were murdered in 1483, after all, which is several years before Christopher Columbus even discovered your part of the world –"

"*We* didn't need discovering!" Jesse shouted from the back. "We already knew where we were!"

The beefeater, fumbling and blushing, realized that Jesse was speaking as a Cree, and he apologized profusely before going on with his story of the two princes.

"We do, however, have a book here that shows a painting of the two young boys. Would you like to see that?"

"Yes!" the Owls shouted.

"Yes, *please!*" shouted Sam and Sarah in unison.

The beefeater made his way to an old bookcase with glazed doors, opened it up, and pulled out a large and somewhat dusty art book. He carefully opened it and leafed through until he came to the picture he was looking for.

"There we go," he said, standing back.

The Owls crowded around the book, each jockeying for position. Travis heard another gasp from Sam, then a small shout from Sarah.

"*Oh my God!*"

Travis was shorter than most of the other players, and had to wait his turn to see what the others were all reacting to. Finally, Gordie Griffith moved out of the way and Travis was in front of the book.

The two princes were in full royal regalia: feathered hats, swords, fancy colourful clothes. The younger one looked so young and innocent.

The older boy, Edward V, was staring defiantly out of the portrait, his eyes a strong, proud blue, his hair long and curling and blond.

Travis was staring at Edward Rose.

8

"LISTEN UP!" MR. DILLINGER SHOUTED TO THE Owls gathered in the main courtyard of the Tower of London. Several of them were off trying to get a closer look at the hopping ravens, but no one dared reach out to touch one.

"Listen up!" Mr. Dillinger repeated. "Every-one over here – on the double!"

The Owls gradually moved in closer to Mr. Dillinger and Muck, suddenly aware that their coach and general manager had been joined by another man: Mr. Wolfe, the yellow-toothed organizer from International In-Line. He was grinning widely, a small foam beach of spittle already on his lower lip.

Travis had no idea what was going on.

"We have some wonderful news for you young Horny Owls . . ."

"*Screech Owls!*" Sam screamed at the top of her lungs.

But it was too late. Nish was off like a balloon that had been blown up and let go untied. He roared with laughter and fell to the ground, rolling about on the short grass while he shouted out, "*Horny Owls! Horny Owls! I love it! I love it! Horny Owls!*"

"Sorry," Mr. Wolfe said, scowling angrily at Nish, who was being nudged by the toe of Muck's boot and had suddenly gone quiet. "Sorry," he repeated. "*Screeeech* Owls," he said, with dripping sarcasm. "You *Screeeech* Owls have been granted permission, along with the Young Lions of Wembley, to spend Wednesday night in a special sleepover at the Tower of London."

"*No way!*" Fahd shouted.

"Yes, yes," Mr. Wolfe sputtered. "My company, International In-Line, has been able to arrange with the powers-that-be, with the much-appreciated help of the Canadian embassy, for the two young teams, as a goodwill gesture, to have an experience never to be forgotten. We'll be sleeping in the Garden Tower. It will get great coverage for our upcoming exhibition match. All the papers will cover it. The BBC will be there . . ."

But Travis was already tuning out. He was thinking about that phrase, "Garden Tower," and wondering where he had just heard it mentioned. Garden Tower . . . Garden Tower . . .

Yes, he remembered. That was its old, formal name. The Garden Tower had been known by another name since the murder of the boy princes.

The *Bloody* Tower.

47

9

THE OWLS WERE ALMOST TOO EXCITED TO CON-
centrate on practice.

The boys were all talking about the Bloody
Tower and how neat it was going to be to sleep
there. The girls were wild about the uncanny
resemblance between the Young Lions star centre
and poor young prince Edward, for whom every
female on the team had now expressed her
undying and total love.

"You're swooning over *dust*!" Nish laughed
when he caught Sam hugging a postcard of the
portrait of the young princes. "He's been *dead* for
over five hundred years!"

"Edward was *valiant*," Sam snapped at
him. "You don't even know what the word
means!"

"Sure I do!"

"What then?"

"I dunno — 'brave'?"

"It's *way* more than that!" Sam hissed, her face
almost as red as Nish's. "It's about being incredi-
bly brave and having grace and knowing what has
to be done and doing it!"

"That's *bull* — you don't even know what happened."

"His brother was smothered with a pillow. Edward was stabbed by his jailers. It's obvious he came to his brother's rescue even though he knew what would happen. That's valiant."

"You don't know that," Nish countered. "They didn't have surveillance cameras in those days."

"I know in my heart what happened," Sam said, near to tears. "And in my heart Edward was valiant, something you'll never understand."

Nish laughed. "Like I *want* to be stabbed. What are you, nuts?"

"Drop it, Nish," Travis warned, pulling his friend's arm to get him into another part of the dressing room away from Sam and Sarah.

"They're *pathetic*," Nish snapped as he let Travis lead him off. "They think they're in love with a ghost."

"Let it go. We've got some practising to do."

Muck had arranged for extra time at the practice facility at the Serpentine. He and Mr. Dillinger and Data had a number of drills to work on, and they put the Owls through their paces for more than an hour: wind sprints, stops and starts, crossovers, two-player rushes, three-player rushes, two-on-ones, three-on-twos, breakouts, penalty killing, and power play.

Travis worked the power play, but Muck made one change, putting Dmitri at centre, where he'd never played, and moving Sarah over to right wing. "This is a speed-through-the-centre game," Muck said. "I want our breaks to come straight up ice and our playmakers along the boards, understand?"

They didn't, but they all nodded as if they did. Muck also switched Sam and Nish so they'd have a left shot on the right side and a right shot on the left. Since there was no blueline, Muck reasoned, there was no point in trying to have players on defence with their sticks tight to the boards. Better, he figured, to have the shot on the open side for a better angle.

Data had a contribution as well. He had dummied up some plays on his laptop to show the Owls.

"I compared video of Owls ice-hockey games to some digital shots of the in-line game against the Young Lions," said Data, delighted to have everyone's rapt attention. "Watch these two examples."

Data's hand flew over the keys and up came some video of Sarah, during a league game back in Tamarack, skating full speed after a player in possession of the puck, only to have Nish's stick lunge into the frame and poke-check the puck. Sarah turned instantly in a massive spray of snow and headed back up ice with the puck.

"Now this," said Data, bringing up his next example.

It was Sarah again, only this time on in-line skates during the practice match against the Young Lions. She was moving down the playing surface in pursuit of Edward Rose, who was carrying the ball.

Nish hit Edward Rose just as he tried to cut for the net – the Owls gathered around the laptop cheering as if they were watching the game live – and Sarah cut hard to turn back with the ball, her skates skipping on the surface as she leaned hard to change direction.

"What do you notice?" Data asked as he killed the screen.

"Sarah's lost a step," Nish said, giggling.

"You're right. You can't turn as quickly on wheels. That makes turnovers a completely different game. And Muck's got a few ideas on that . . ."

Muck then talked about how the Owls were going to attack from now on. He wanted them to think about soccer, and about lacrosse, and he wanted them to keep circling as they mounted an attack rather than always going for the fast break.

"If the fast break is there for you," said Muck, "fine. Take it. But if you're trying to move the puck" – Muck coughed, uncomfortable – ". . . or whatever they call that silly thing . . . if you're trying to move it up, you want to do it in waves."

"Swedish hockey!" Lars shouted.

"Classic Russian hockey," Dmitri corrected.

"Why?" asked Fahd.

"If we can get them chasing us, going toward our net," said Muck, "then when we move it forward they'll have to turn. And I think every time we can drop back and drop back and then attack fast, we can catch them going the wrong way. And by the time they'll have turned, we'll be in on them."

"I like it," said Dmitri.

"I *love* it," said Lars, who was forever singing the praises of European hockey and telling them they could learn something from soccer.

"We'll try it," said Muck.

He split the Owls into two teams for a prolonged scrimmage. Every time the players followed their normal hockey instincts – to head-man the ball, to look for the fast break, to charge straight ahead – Muck's whistle blew. Not to stop play, but to remind the players to reverse fields, to circle back, send lateral passes across the surface, do whatever was necessary to get the other side to stop skating back to receive the attack and lure them forward to try to gain control of the ball.

The moment the tide turned and the side not in possession of the ball began moving forward, Muck wanted the side in possession to charge straight ahead, forcing the defenders to turn.

It worked. Dmitri and Lars instantly under-stood the thinking behind the new style of play.

Sarah caught on quickly too, and gradually the entire team understood this new form of attack: wait, circle, wait again, draw the other side toward you, then charge.

Travis's line played wonderfully in the new system, thanks largely to the move that put Dmitri at centre and in charge of the attack patterns. Sarah adapted nicely to her new role, and Travis found that he, too, could play better if he just showed the patience that seemed to come so naturally to Dmitri and Lars.

By the end of an hour they were exhausted and itchy with sweat. Nish's face was so wet and red it seemed on the verge of bursting. But he towelled off quickly, yanked out his new helmet, and pulled it on as if he'd just been awarded the MVP prize.

They undressed in silence, tossing their soaked jerseys into a pile in the centre of the tent for Mr. Dillinger to pick up for washing, the only sound the rip and tear of the shin-pad tape coming off and being tossed over to Sam's corner so she could wrap it onto her growing ball.

Finally, Nish broke the silence.

"Can we *please* get rid of that stupid ball?" he said, his voice slightly muffled.

"What's your problem, Big Boy?" Sam asked.

"It's embarrassing – you make us look like a. . . ."

"Like a what?" Sarah said, pouncing. "Like a *girl's* team?"

Nish was scarlet. "I didn't say that."

"No, but that's what you think," said Liz.

"I just think it's time to drop it," Nish said. "It's too big. It's out of control."

"Like you," said Jenny.

Nish shrugged. "I hate it," he said. "You won't get any of my tape."

"We don't want your tape!" Sam snapped, picking up her tape ball and ramming it deep inside her equipment bag. "Besides, we think your stupid golden helmet's embarrassing. I wouldn't be caught dead wearing something like that."

Nish shrieked. "You don't have to worry! It's for the best player on each team – and we all know who that is, don't we?"

Sam threw some loose shin-pad tape at Nish, who let it bounce harmlessly off his prize helmet.

Travis went back to untying his skates. He could not believe how silly some arguments could get. He remembered his dad once saying that when he had been a young boy they used to say things like "Your mother wears army boots" to upset someone in the schoolyard – and it worked!

Talk changes, Travis thought, but not the stupidity of it.

He wasn't embarrassed by the tape ball one bit.

He was often embarrassed by his best friend.

10

TRAVIS WAS ALMOST OVERWHELMED BY THE
bustle.

The Screech Owls had gone for another tour.
This time they walked down through Hyde
Park in a light drizzle so that Muck could have
Data take his picture standing underneath the
Wellington Arch, and then the team carried on
across Green Park toward Buckingham Palace.

The warm rain let up just as the changing
of the guard outside the palace began. Travis
found the formal, scheduled procession less interesting than what was going on all around.

Along the length of the wide pinkish-paved
avenue called The Mall, the police were erecting
barriers. There were seating stands being ham-
mered up near the fountain opposite the palace
and even more stands going up in front of Canada
Gate to the right of the main palace gates.

Simon pointed out that the structures looked
just like hockey stands.

"I thought we were playing at some place
called Wembley!" cracked Nish.

But the special seating and the barriers had nothing to do with any peewee hockey team from Canada. It was all for the procession that the Queen and the rest of the royal family would be making along The Mall and down the twisting Horse Guards Road to Westminster Pier, where they would board a yacht that would carry them along the Thames to the Tower of London.

Travis found it hard to imagine such a fuss being made over some jewels. Travis once had a rock collection, and he cried when his mother accidentally threw it out, but this was different. This was an entire city going mad over a few shiny stones.

For days, the television news and the London papers had been talking about little else but the seven hundredth anniversary of the Crown Jewels being in the Tower of London. There were photographs of a sword covered in rubies, several pictures of what the newspapers were calling the largest diamond in the world, and a full-page spread of the crown the Queen would put on, briefly, once she had arrived at the Tower: the Imperial State Crown, which, one television reporter said, glittered with 2,868 diamonds, 273 pearls, seventeen sapphires, eleven emeralds, and five rubies.

Some rock collection, Travis thought.

"It's not about jewels," Muck told them when Travis asked why people would get so worked up about a crown. "It's about symbolism. It's about longevity. It says that the world can change, an empire can rise and fall, centuries can pass, and yet the Crown carries on. People here would say it stands for British civilization, even if a bunch of people in Canada think it's rather silly to have a Queen. It isn't silly over here, believe me."

Muck seemed almost transformed by this trip, Travis thought. The old coach's eyes took on a new glow whenever he came across a statue or a war memorial or a museum. There was almost a light step to his walk, even though Muck's limp was obvious whenever they went on a long walk through the parks.

After they had watched the changing of the guard at Buckingham Palace and walked around to see all the preparations for the royal procession, Muck took them to Kensington, where he put Mr. Dillinger in charge of leading the Owls through the Natural History Museum so they could see the dinosaur collection. Muck himself was off to the nearby Victoria and Albert Museum, where, he said, he planned to look at the special exhibition of Renaissance furniture.

"After that," Nish asked, "do you suppose we could go somewhere and watch paint dry?"

Muck didn't even bother to acknowledge the wisecrack. He was used to Nish. He was also used to the kids wondering how anyone so caught up in the fast game of hockey could at the same time be obsessed with something so slow it no longer even moved: history.

But none of them had ever figured out Muck, and none of them expected they ever would.

He was just Muck – and they wouldn't want him any other way.

Back at the hotel, they were given thirty minutes to pack up for the bus that would take them to the Tower of London for the special overnight stay.

Mr. Wolfe, the snaggle-toothed human water-hose was there to organize everyone. He was so wound up, it struck Travis it would be a lot easier if Mr. Wolfe had stayed out of the way.

But Mr. Wolfe had his own good reasons for being there.

"We want you to bring all your stuff along," he announced, spittle spraying. "There will be storage space made available in one of the other towers for your hockey equipment. You can bring your suitcases to the sleeping quarters in the Garden Tower, where we'll be."

"He means Bloody Tower," whispered Fahd. "He just doesn't want to say it."

Maybe, Travis thought, it was just another case of absent-mindedness.

Travis was thinking about something else. He saw what Mr. Wolfe was up to. He wanted them moved completely out of their hotel for the night so that the rooms could be rented out to the tourists who were still flooding into London for the royal procession. They'd be willing to pay top price, and that would add up to a lot of money if the rooms were available. Mr. Wolfe was making certain they would be.

"We'll be putting the Young Lions on the middle floor," Mr. Wolfe was saying. "The Grey Owls will be up top –"

"*SCREECH!*" Sam screeched.

"Sorry, Screech Owls," Mr. Wolfe apologized.

But Travis wasn't even listening. He was wondering just how well off Mr. Wolfe's company was. They were gambling that by getting some public attention, in-line skating and in-line hockey would somehow take off in Great Britain. But if they were already trying to cut corners, what did that say about their future?

Travis decided it wasn't his concern. He didn't have to worry about the company's future. And he couldn't really blame Mr. Wolfe for trying to regain some of the hotel costs while the team was being put up, free of charge, at the Tower of London. So long as the airline tickets home were valid and the Owls made it back to Tamarack, it really didn't matter one way or the other to Travis.

Besides, he couldn't stand Mr. Wolfe. He wouldn't be bothered in the least to see this pompous, full-of-himself spitter fall flat on his face. In fact, he'd be delighted.

Travis surprised himself with his own animosity toward Mr. Wolfe. After all, he didn't even really know the man.

"Can I bring my golden helmet?" Nish asked, putting on his best choirboy look for good measure.

Mr. Wolfe smiled widely, bad teeth and all.

"Of course, Mr. Nikabama . . ."

"*NISH-I-KA-WA!*" Sam shouted, stomping her feet.

"Nishikawa," Mr. Wolfe repeated, still smiling. "We *want* you to bring it, young man. We might get some good media out of this. I've asked young Mr. Rose to bring his along as well. Just imagine the photo op!"

Nish beamed, turning and bowing slightly to his teammates on either side of him as if he'd just been knighted by the Queen. "Can I wear it?"

Mr. Wolfe finally laughed at something that wasn't his own joke. "Of course you can, lad – wear it as you're walking into the Tower if you like."

"Geez," Nish said, a strong blush working up his face. "Thanks, Mr. Wolfe."

"My pleasure, sonny. My pleasure."

Travis thought he may have misjudged Mr. Wolfe. Maybe he really did have his heart in the right place.

11

"YOU LOOK LIKE AN IDIOT!"

Travis didn't mince his words. He didn't much like being so sharp with a teammate, but he was, after all, captain of the team, and Nish was making a spectacle of the Owls.

"Mr. Wolfe *said* I could wear it!" came the muffled response.

The Screech Owls were lined up to enter the Tower of London. Muck and Mr. Dillinger were hanging back – almost, Travis thought, as if they were trying to distance themselves from the team – and the rest of the Owls were careful to stand a couple of paces behind the team captain, Travis, and the very first Screech Owl in line. Wayne Nishikawa, the Kid in the Golden Hockey Helmet.

Travis had his packsack over one shoulder and was carrying Data's laptop in his other hand. The in-line hockey equipment had already been whisked off by the Tower of London staff and stashed in a supply room for the night. Now the team was lining up to go through security.

How everything had changed in a mere two days. There had been security during their previous tour of the Tower, but apart from the surveillance cameras at the entrance, it had amounted to just a quick check of their bags.

Now it was worse than an airport.

Fahd was the first to notice the men on the rooftops as they got off the bus on Tower Hill. Data identified them as army sharpshooters getting their bearings for tomorrow's royal procession to the Tower of London.

There seemed to be dark figures moving stealthily over every rooftop within sight, even on the ancient All Hallows by the Tower church that stood on the grounds far to their right.

"There will be cops everywhere tomorrow," Data said. "The Queen will be driven up from the pier in an open car. Those things are a nightmare for security."

This was a nightmare, thought Travis. A team of peewee hockey players from Canada – twelve- and thirteen-year-old kids from a small town called Tamarack – and they were being treated like potential hijackers as they worked their way through the new security precautions at the Tower of London.

There were crowd-control barriers all along the roadsides. There were fenced-in stands facing the front gate where the Queen's car would arrive. There were police milling about everywhere, several of them armed. There were new surveillance cameras installed. And there was a large metal-detector machine that everyone had to file through and *then* be subjected to more checks with a detector wand as well as physical checks of every bag being carried into the building.

There would also be random strip searches, Mr. Wolfe had warned the Owls.

"*Let Nish do it!*" Sam had shouted from the back of the bus. "*He'll volunteer!*"

"*Shut your trap!*" Nish had snapped, delighted, from inside his ridiculous helmet.

Now the security staff was ready to process the Owls. Nish would be first. He stood in line, grinning out from under his unusual helmet while a young soldier in fatigues looked at him once, then twice, then a third time with a puzzled look.

"You are, sir?" the soldier asked.

"Wayne Nishikawa!" Nish's muffled voice announced. "N-I-S-H-I-K –"

"Yes, sir," the soldier said, ticking off the name on his clipboarded list of admissible visitors. "I can spell quite all right, sir." The soldier looked up, blinking. "Excuse me, sir," he said. "But is *that*" – he pointed at the helmet with the eraser of his pencil – "because of some medical condition?"

"If you mean *insanity*," Sam cracked from back in the line, "you guessed it!"

Nish waved her off with a backward flutter of his hand. "It's the award for being top player on the team," said Nish.

Travis couldn't see if Nish was blushing. He didn't need to.

"I see," said the soldier. "Would you take it off, sir?"

"*I can't bring it in?*" Nish yelped.

"We just want to put it through the X-ray machine, sir. You can have it right back."

Reluctantly, Nish removed his treasured helmet and handed it to the soldier, who examined it by hand before laying it down on the conveyer belt moving through the X-ray machine.

"*Put his head back in it!*" Sam called to the soldier. "*We want to see if there's anything inside!*"

Nish's hair was wet with sweat, and his face even redder than usual. Travis wondered how he could stand wearing that helmet for so long.

Nish moved ahead through the metal detector. Travis handed his bag and Data's laptop over to the soldier, who placed them on the conveyor belt, and followed Nish. There was no sound, and the soldier holding the detector wand waved him forward.

Another soldier picked up the laptop and opened it. He pushed the on button and waited for the screen to light up. Satisfied, he then handed it to yet another soldier, who took a black plastic pointer with a small white cloth attached to the end and ran the cloth over the keys, the screen, and the outsides of the small computer.

"What's that for?" Travis asked.

The soldier smiled as she plucked off the white cloth and placed it in a machine and pushed a series of buttons. "We can detect explosives with this," she said. "We turn on the screen to make sure it's really a computer and not a false case, then check to ensure no one ever handled gun powder or anything around it."

"What if you found something?" Travis asked her.

She smiled again. "Then you, young man, would be in big, big trouble."

"It's not mine," he said.

She smiled again. "That's what they always say."

The machine beeped once and a green light came on. The soldier handed Travis the computer with a nice smile. "We'll let you go this time, okay?"

"Thanks," Travis said, taking the computer and moving on, impressed with the thoroughness of the security check.

If they were this careful with a peewee hockey team, he thought, then imagine how closely they checked everyone else.

12

THE YOUNG LIONS OF WEMBLEY WERE ALREADY
in the courtyard. There were name tags for everyone – "Hello," Travis's read, "My name is Travis"
– and the two teams lined up to shake hands and
introduce each other. Sam and Sarah ran back to
get in line so they could shake Edward Rose's
hand twice, much to the disgust of Nish, who
had his helmet back on.

Edward Rose, to his credit, was not wearing
his golden helmet, but Travis noticed that it was
hooked onto one of the backpacks that the
Young Lions had piled against one of the stone
walls. Mr. Wolfe must have suggested to him, too,
that he bring it along for the "photo op."

"Travis Lindsay," Travis said automatically as he
came to the outstretched hand of Edward Rose.

Edward Rose smiled brilliantly, blue eyes
dancing with recognition. "Aha," he said, "the
nifty little captain. You're a good one, mate. I'm
Edward Rose."

Travis felt his resistance melt away. Edward
Rose might be full of himself. He might look like
the young murdered prince with his long blond

hair and blue eyes, but he wasn't so full of himself that he was unaware of the world about him. He had noticed Travis during the match and remembered his name.

Nifty little captain.

Travis didn't much care for the "little" part, but he loved being called "nifty."

The beefeaters gave the two peewee teams a tour unlike any other. It had nothing to do with the usual tourist stuff like the Crown Jewels and the history of who was imprisoned in which tower when, and everything to do with what twelve- and thirteen-year-old kids wanted to see.

They were shown where the moat and drawbridge once were at the front gate.

They were shown the tower where one of the kings kept his lions and leopard and even an elephant and a white bear.

They were shown where the scaffold once stood on Tower Hill and how tens of thousands of people would assemble there for public executions – "cheering, if you can believe it, just like they would at a football game."

"Hockey game," corrected Nish.

"Hockey game," the good-natured beefeater with the twirled grey moustache agreed. "Only no one ever loses their head at a hockey game now, do they?"

"You've never seen Nish play, then!" shot Sam.

"Does anyone here know what tomorrow is?" the beefeater asked.

"The royal procession," said Fahd.

"Correct," the beefeater said. "But it's also something else very special. Any guesses?"

Edward Rose spoke up. "Guy Fawkes Day."

"Not fair, young fella – you're an Englishman. But yes, Guy Fawkes Day. Like your Hallowe'en in Canada."

"That was last week," said Wilson.

"Yes, but tomorrow night, November the fifth, boys and girls all over England will be getting old clothes and stuffing them with straw to make a life-size man and then taking him door to door asking, 'A penny for the Guy, please?'"

"You can't *eat* pennies!" Nish cracked.

The beefeater paid no attention. "Then," he said, "later in the evening, there will be bonfires all through the countryside and the kids will throw their Guys on the fire and set off fireworks and chant a little rhyme. Go on now" – he peered at the name tag on Edward Rose – "Mr. Rose, tell our Canadian visitors what it is."

Edward Rose blushed, but chanted out in a clear voice:

> *Please to remember*
> *The fifth of November*
> *Gunpowder, treason, and plot*
> *We know of no reason*

Why gunpowder treason
Should ever be forgot.

"Excellent, my young man. Excellent."

"Excuse me," said Fahd, a puzzled look on his face, "but why would you celebrate a man who tried to blow up your Houses of Parliament?"

"Well," the beefeater chuckled, "there's always been a great many who wish he'd succeeded. But seriously, young man, there are those who say we should never forget in order that we all recognize how fortunate we are to have our type of government and our good Queen. Guy Fawkes is not a hero, but a villain in British history, and people should never forget their history. Guy Fawkes needs to be *remembered*."

"We remember — we saw what he looked like before they split him apart," said Derek.

"Ah," the beefeater said, twirling his moustache, "then you've visited Madame Tussaud's. Well, what you wouldn't have learned there, though, is that Guy Fawkes was brought here to the Tower when he was captured. He was taken directly to the chamber inside the Queen's House that I just showed to you, and there he was made to confess — you can use your imaginations to think how that might have been done — and it was here that he named his co-conspirators. So you are standing in exactly the same courtyard that Guy Fawkes once walked through. How about that?"

"Neat," said Willie.

"Freaky," said Liz.

"Creepy," said Jesse.

"Now," the beefeater announced, "would you like to help us feed the ravens?"

Travis felt strange holding a blood-soaked biscuit in his hand. He wondered what blood it was — beef? pork? . . . *human?* — and whether the ritual had changed over the centuries.

One of the ravens was hopping aggressively toward Travis. "That'd be Hardey, mate," the beefeater said to Travis. "He's the oldest and expects special treatment. I wouldn't deny him, now. You just flip that delicious little morsel in the air and see what happens."

Travis had no intention of trying to feed one of these pecking machines by hand. He tossed the biscuit so it looped through the air, and Hardey, with practised timing, leaped up and snatched it in mid-flight.

"*Nice catch!*" Travis shouted.

"He'd answer you back," the smiling beefeater said, "but his mouth's kind of full."

Hardey gorged himself on the treat and began hopping aggressively again toward Travis, who retreated instinctively, causing the beefeater to chuckle.

Everywhere Travis looked, he could see kids feeding the ravens under the watchful eye of a warden. Some, like Sam, were determined to befriend the fierce black birds and waited until the last moment before releasing the blood-soaked biscuit.

The beefeater with Travis was naming the ravens by sight, even at a considerable distance, pointing them out for Travis's benefit.

"That be Gomer, he's a fighter. And Hugine . . . and that there is Odin . . . there we have Munin . . . hmmmmm."

Travis heard a note of wonder in the beef-eater's voice. "What?" he asked.

The beefeater kept twirling his moustache, his eyes darting over the lawn and courtyard. "I don't see Thor . . . or Cedric . . . That's odd."

He had not been the only one to notice. Two other beefeaters were glancing about the court-yard, trying to account for all the birds. Both turned, looks of surprise in their faces, and came walking toward the older beefeater.

"Cedric's missing," one of them said. "Not like him to miss his bloody biscuit."

"And Thor," the other said. "There's two didn't show."

"I don't like five," the grey-moustached beefeater said. "I don't like five at all – and par-ticularly not this week."

The three beefeaters stood watching the kids feed the birds, each of them still scanning about for the two missing ravens while Travis frantically searched through his memory for what "five" might mean.

There were five ravens being fed, and two missing – Thor and Cedric.

What was the rule?

The king – Charles something? – had decreed there must always be how many ravens at the Tower of London?

Then he remembered.

Six ravens at the Tower of London or the Crown would fall.

But now there were only five.

And why was that particularly bad this week?

Of course, Travis realized, his heart suddenly pounding in his chest.

The Queen was coming!

13

THE TWO TEAMS RETURNED TO THE BLOODY Tower to find their packs had already been taken up to the large empty rooms in which they'd be camping out on thin, self-inflatable sleeping pads and bags, all thoughtfully supplied by International In-Line.

Travis hadn't said anything to anyone about the ravens. It was silly, he figured, to wonder where the two missing birds might be when, for all he knew, they were simply in another part of the Tower complex begging food from tourists. And as for the omen that the Crown was about to fall . . . he'd look pretty silly saying that in front of the team. Kidders like Sam and Nish would never let him live it down.

Still, he couldn't help but worry. Worrying came naturally to Travis Lindsay, and he was simply being true to his nature. But he would worry *alone*. Besides, he figured he was capable of doing enough of it for everyone.

"*Someone took my helmet!*" Nish hissed in Travis's ear.

Travis snapped out of his reverie. "Huh?"

"Someone took the golden helmet," Nish repeated. "It's gone. It was with my pack. Now there's nothing there!"

Travis, the captain, knew what was required. He would have to take charge. "No one took it," he said. "They just piled it somewhere else, that's all."

But Nish wasn't buying it. He was red-faced and angry. "I wouldn't put it past that Sam to hide it someplace."

Travis looked around them. "Where? Hide it where? There's no place here that she'd be able to hide it without the wardens seeing her. Besides, she's not that way."

"Is too," hissed Nish.

"C'mon," Travis said. "I'll help you look for it."

They searched all around the room, but could find it nowhere. Nish was growing more and more angry, but Travis talked him into staying quiet about it until they searched the courtyard to see if it had been left behind by accident.

With Mr. Dillinger's permission, the two Owls made their way down the stone spiral staircase to the front door of the Bloody Tower and out into the walkway that took them to the main courtyard.

They checked everywhere. They asked three of the beefeaters on duty if perhaps they had seen it or, for that matter, seen someone take it, but no one had noticed anything. One beefeater told Nish not to worry, that no one would steal anything in here. It just wouldn't happen.

"I'm not talking about 'stealing,'" Nish said to Travis as they walked away disappointed. "I'm talking about Sam jacking me around for the fun of it."

"Well," said Travis, "then we'll just have to ask her, won't we?"

But Sam knew nothing. "Never saw it, never touched it," she said firmly. "*Wouldn't* touch it."

Nish was adamant. "Who did, then? *Somebody* made off with it."

"Not me, Big Boy – nice try, but not me."

Sarah's voice called from across the room. "Is *this* what you're looking for?" She was standing with Nish's helmet in her hands, staring in wonder at them.

"Give me that!" Nish said, hurrying over to snatch it away from Sarah.

"Where'd you find it?" Travis asked, smiling with delight that the mystery was solved.

"It was sitting on his pack!" Sarah giggled.

"*Not a chance!*" said Nish.

"I swear. I heard you asking Sam and walked straight over and picked it up. Just ask Fahd."

Fahd, who'd come up behind Sarah, was nodding in agreement.

Nish's face was now almost scarlet. His mouth was wide open in disbelief, nothing coming out of it for once.

"It wasn't there when we checked," said Travis.

Sarah shrugged. "Well, it's a mystery."

"I guess," said Travis.

Nish didn't care. He had his beloved helmet back and was hauling it on over his thick black hair. He jiggled it around, yanked it off, banged it a couple of times, pushed the face mask hard into the helmet, and pulled it on again. "*Damn!*" he shouted, not caring who heard him swear.

"What's wrong?" said Travis.

"Whoever took it wrecked it!" Nish wailed. "It doesn't fit any more!"

14

THEY WERE PLUCKING AT TRAVIS'S EYES!

His head was no longer connected to his body. It had been stabbed onto a pole and the pole jammed into the ground at the foot of Tower Bridge.

There was a raven on his forehead, leaning over to pluck at his eyes again!

I'm still alive! Travis screamed.

His brain was okay. He could see everything: the bridge, the river barges floating by with their loads of garbage, people in fancy clothes walking along below, pointing at him and laughing.

And he could shout. *"Save me! Get me down from here!"* But no one seemed to hear him.

He could feel the blood dripping out of his ears. He looked up, blinking, as the heavy beak of the cawing black bird got ready to rip at his eyeball.

It was Cedric!

Another raven screamed hideously as it came in for a landing on Travis's hair.

Thor! It was Thor!

The missing ravens from the Tower of London were here! They weren't lost! The Crown was saved!

Travis tried to shout out to the beefeaters he saw walking across the bridge, but none of them paid the slightest attention. He screamed, but they were too busy talking, too busy laughing.

Then the bridge began filling with faces he knew. Nish with his enormous golden hockey helmet, now bigger than a hot-air balloon. Sam and Sarah walking arm in arm with Edward Rose.

"Sarah! Help me! Sam! Can you hear me?"

But they paid him no heed. Not even a flicker of recognition as they stood and looked out over the spiked heads of thieves and traitors and pointed to all the skulls and eye-picking ravens and the freshly beheaded Travis Lindsay.

"Noooooooo!" Travis screamed. *"I'm innocent!"*

But it did no good. They were pointing at him and laughing.

Sam pulled out her disposable camera and aimed it right at Travis's bleeding, spiked head, laughing while she composed the shot and raised her finger over the button.

Flash!!!

The light filled the room, causing groans all around.

"No school today!" Nish mumbled from the sleeping bag beside Travis's.

Travis shook off his nightmare. His heart was pounding. His face was hot. He was covered in sweat.

He kicked off the heavy sleeping bag and lay there for a minute, feeling the lovely cooling sensation as the sweat evaporated from his body. His pyjamas felt damp now, and he'd be glad to be out of them and dressed.

The light had been turned on by Mr. Wolfe, who was standing at the doorway with a big crooked-toothed smile. He spat out his announcement.

"Morning, Young Lions and Barred Owls . . ."

"*Screech!*" Sam howled from beneath her sleeping bag.

"Sorry about that," Mr. Wolfe said. But he didn't sound sorry at all. "We have a light breakfast prepared for everyone down below, and then I'm afraid we have to clear out so they can get ready for the royal visit. We've been offered a prime spot along the parade route to watch them arrive, and I have accepted on your behalf."

A small cheer went up for Mr. Wolfe, who seemed to be making just a bit too much of his role. The players all knew that everyone in London had been invited to join in the celebration of the Crown Jewels, so it was hardly as if the Queen herself had declared she would not go unless she could be promised that the Screech Owls of Canada and the Young Lions of

Wembley would be there to wave back at her.

"Up and at it, then," Mr. Wolfe said. "I trust you all had a good night."

Apart from the nightmare, Travis had. They had stayed up late talking hockey with the other team and everyone had gotten along splendidly. They watched a short film about the Tower of London and they cheered every time they saw a familiar face in it. The ravens, of course, got the loudest cheers of all.

The ravens . . . yes, the ravens, Travis thought. He wondered if Thor and Cedric had turned up.

Thank heaven they weren't really sitting on his spiked head dining on his eyeballs!

Travis and Nish sat with Sam and Sarah over a breakfast of cold cereal, cold toast, and lukewarm orange juice. It wasn't the best, but it was filling, and Travis was starved.

They had just sat down when Edward Rose strolled over, his breakfast on a tray, and asked if he could join them.

"Sure," said Sam. "By all means."

Travis could not help but notice that she was blushing almost as deeply as Nish sometimes did.

Nish, however, was more curious about what Edward Rose had on his tray. "You drink coffee?"

Edward Rose laughed. "No, mate – it's tea."

"*Tea?*" Nish practically choked. "My *mother* drinks tea!" He said it as if the drink could somehow turn Edward Rose into a middle-aged woman taking a break from her gardening.

"Well, then," he said, without taking the slightest offence, "I think your mother has good taste. I love tea."

"I like hot chocolate," Travis offered, then immediately felt silly.

"Muck says there's only one thing wrong with London," Sarah giggled, then tried imitating Muck: "Thousands of years of civilization and they can't make a decent cup of coffee."

"What's he want?" Nish said, shaking his head, "a Tim Hortons at Buckingham Palace?"

Sam burst out laughing. "That's *exactly* what he'd like!"

"What's a Tim Hortons?" Edward Rose asked, looking from one to the other with a mystified look.

"He's a hockey player," Nish said.

Edward Rose looked even more puzzled. "Ice hockey? You want an ice hockey player at Buckingham Palace?"

"Never mind," laughed Sam. "It's too complicated to explain."

Travis decided to change the subject. "Someone took Nish's helmet and wrecked it," he said.

Edward Rose, who was in the middle of sipping his tea, suddenly started to splutter.

"Too hot?" Travis asked.

"No. It's what you said about your helmet."

"What?" Nish asked. "Someone took *yours*?"

"Yes. I don't know who, though. And then it mysteriously turned up again."

"Let's go look at it," said Travis.

Together, the five peewee players wandered over to where the Young Lions' things had been piled up, ready to go. They could see the golden helmet almost immediately, dangling from a clip on Edward Rose's packsack.

Edward unclipped it and held it up, examining it carefully. "Seems fine to me," he declared.

"Put it on," said Nish.

"Did you try it on before?" asked Sam.

"Yes, once," Edward Rose said, sounding almost embarrassed. "Mr. Wolfe asked if I would bring it along for photo ops – the BBC was supposed to be here, but I never saw anyone."

"Put it on," Nish said again.

Edward Rose looked once more at the helmet, then unstrapped it and lifted it up over his head and placed it on his mane of yellow hair.

He shook his head, his eyes puzzled.

He pulled off the helmet and stared inside, mystified.

"It's too loose now," he said.

"Same jerk who wrecked mine," said Nish, disgusted. "Same pumpkin-headed jerk."

15

THE DAY WAS WARM, A SOFT MIST BURNING OFF the Thames as the teams boarded their buses outside the Tower of London, the Owls headed back to their hotel, the Young Lions for their various homes. The two teams were to meet up later to watch the royal procession.

The big exhibition match would be held the next night at the world-famous Wembley Stadium. Wembley, where the World Cup of soccer had been held . . . where the Olympic torch had been lit to open the 1948 Olympic Games . . . where the most-famous ice hockey team in Great Britain, the Wembley Lions, had played their games.

And now, where the Young Lions of Wembley would meet the Screech Owls of Tamarack to decide . . . well, to decide nothing, really. It was just an exhibition match to showcase a sport that didn't even have a world championship, a sport that hardly anyone in the world cared about, except for a bunch of kids from England and Canada.

They might call it an exhibition match, Travis decided, but to the players it would be the Stanley

Cup of in-line hockey, even if not a soul came to watch.

It was impossible to say if there was any interest in the match among Londoners. There had been no mention in the papers, and Mr. Wolfe's promised feature on BBC television, to be shot at the Tower, had never come off.

All that the people were interested in was the royal procession to the Tower of London anyway. The papers were filled with stories and photographs of the spectacular Crown Jewels. All of Britain, it seemed, was caught up in the seven hundredth anniversary celebration. One columnist wrote that the jewel-encrusted sword alone would get the homeless off the street if it were sold; another wrote that the collection was the ultimate symbol of the monarchy, and therefore of the government itself; and the television stations were all boasting that their coverage would be the best and most thorough of the late-afternoon affair.

Muck wanted the Owls to work the stiffness out of their limbs after their night of sleeping on the floor. He told them to get dressed in their track suits and then gather in the hotel lobby. Sarah and Travis would lead the team on a run down the Edgware Road and through the underpass to Hyde Park, where Muck wanted them to follow the paths and around the Serpentine and back via the Ring Road.

Muck and Mr. Dillinger would meet them again at Marble Arch.

No one made a crack about Muck not running. There wasn't a player on the team that didn't know the story about Muck's bad leg and how, but for the break, he would have gone on to the National Hockey League. And as for Mr. Dillinger, well, he was simply too heavy to run farther than the corner where the Edgware Road began, let alone all the way down to the park and back.

With Travis and Sarah in charge, the team loped down the street at an easy pace, careful not to forget the traffic wasn't going the way they were used to, and equally careful not to bother any of the pedestrians, many of whom were young mothers pushing baby carriages.

They ran easily, and soon burst up out of the underpass into a park still green and lush with late-season growth.

Travis sucked in the smells, revelling in a sense of the outdoors he never expected in such a huge city. He felt as if he were running in Tamarack, heading toward the school and the arena. As far as he could see was green, green grass. The huge trees with their yellowing leaves blocked any view of the city, and as they turned down toward the ponds it seemed they weren't in a city at all.

Sarah led for a while and then Travis. Dmitri, the best runner on the Owls, took over after a time. He stepped up the pace, and Nish and Sam dropped back, talking together as they ran.

Travis, who had turned to run backwards for a bit, took note of this and wondered how it was that Nish and Sam could act like they hated each other's guts and yet at rare times like this seem the greatest of friends.

He already knew he would never understand his best friend. He figured he would never understand Sam, either.

Travis turned back to concentrate on his running. Data had a theory that running was like a computer double-tasking. You could have a computer printing something at the same time you were surfing the Internet for new information, and it sometimes seemed as if the computer was doing two complicated things at once with neither job being aware of the other.

"Your brain is the best computer the world has ever known," Data would say. "Well, perhaps not Nish's. But the human brain can do things when we're not even aware of it. You run and think of running, and the next thing you know your brain is coughing out an answer to a question you didn't even realize you were thinking of."

Travis wondered how Data's mind worked. He marvelled at Data's enormous grasp of information and complicated tasks. The accident with the car that winter had put him in a wheelchair and taken all but partial movement from him, but it sometimes seemed as if Data's terrific brain had stepped in to make up for all the other shortcomings.

Travis had started to count his own steps – "61 ... 62 ... 63 ... 64 ... 65 ... 66 ..." when a thought suddenly popped into his brain as surely as if his tongue had reached up and put it there.

Fox.

He ran a little farther.

"67 ... 68 ... 69 ... 70 ..."

Wolf!

"71 ... 72 ... 73 ..."

Fox?

He started thinking about the phone call he had overheard down by the Serpentine that day after the first match with the Young Lions. He had thought Mr. Wolfe referred to himself as "Fox" out of absent-mindedness.

But what if it was a play on words – or a code name?

What if bumbling Mr. Wolfe was really sly as a fox?

Travis's mind suddenly exploded with con-nections.

Fox! Fawkes!

Fawkes! Fox!

Guy Fawkes!

Travis felt a sharp pain in his side. A stitch.

He couldn't go on. He stopped and bent over to ease the pain.

Sarah held up the rest of the Owls, most of them anxious anyway for an excuse to slow down or stop.

"You okay, Trav?"

Travis didn't answer. He was in too much pain from the stitch, and his brain was reeling with something. It was something important – something terrifying – but he wasn't quite sure what.

He tried breathing deeply, letting the thoughts sort themselves out. Mr. Wolfe had called himself "Fox" when he was on his cellphone, when he thought he was all alone down by the Serpentine. He had said something about the helmets, something about how everything had gone according to plan.

Mr. Wolfe had been the one who handed out the helmets after that first match, special prizes for a game that hadn't even been serious.

Mr. Wolfe had been the one who made sure – heck, *insisted* – that Nish bring along his helmet to the Tower of London for the sleepover.

Mr. Wolfe had asked Edward Rose to make sure he brought his helmet along, too, saying the BBC would be there to shoot a short feature on the two in-line teams – but the BBC had never shown up. *Maybe they never were going to show up.*

Nish's helmet had mysteriously gone missing. Edward Rose's helmet had mysteriously gone missing.

Both helmets had mysteriously been returned to their original place.

Something was wrong with both helmets. Neither one fit any longer. They were too big.

Travis slapped his own head. He couldn't fit it all together! The computer wasn't working properly. There was information here, but he couldn't process it fast enough!

Travis remained bent over, gasping for breath, his mind racing.

"Trav?" Sarah asked again, with growing concern in her voice. "You okay?"

Travis waved her off, afraid to speak for fear it would stop his mind from processing all this material.

Today was Guy Fawkes Day. Today the royal family was off to the Tower of London to celebrate the Crown Jewels.

Mr. Wolfe – Mr. Fox . . . *Mr. Fawkes?* – had spent the night in the Tower with the kids. Travis shook his head. It couldn't be. Could it?

"*Trav?*" Sarah asked, putting her hand gently on his back.

Travis sucked in his wind. He could hardly speak. "We have to get back!" he said.

"But Muck and Mr. Dillinger are meeting us at Marble Arch."

Travis shook his head. "*No time – let's go!*"

16

TRAVIS HAD NEVER RUN SO FAR SO FAST IN ALL his life.

He flew up the Edgware Road and onto George Street, heading for the side entrance to the hotel. He ran straight to his room and grabbed Nish's helmet.

Sarah, Sam, and Dmitri were right behind him, the other Owls still coming along the street, having set off to meet Muck and Mr. Dillinger at Marble Arch and explain.

But explain what? Travis himself did not know. All he was certain of was that there had to be an explanation.

Travis began to yank out the padding of the helmet just as Nish came in, gasping.

"*Hey!*" Nish shouted. "*Don't make it any worse than it is!*"

"There was something here!" Travis said, turning the helmet toward the rest so they could see what he was looking at: nothing.

"What do you mean?" asked Sam. "You're not making any sense."

"Something happened to both helmets to

make them larger. The only explanation is that someone removed some of the padding.

"Why would they do that?" Dmitri asked.

"I don't know," Travis said. "But there's something going on with these helmets. Do you have Edward Rose's number?"

He looked at the girls.

Sarah giggled. "Yes, why?"

"Call him. See if his helmet was tampered with under the padding."

"He'll think we're crazy."

"*I don't care what he thinks*," Travis practically shouted. "*Call him!*"

"Okay, okay. Don't get your underwear in a knot."

"What's all this about?" asked Nish.

"Is Data still here?" Travis shouted.

"He's in the lobby," Fahd said, as he came in puffing for air.

"Let's go!" Travis said. "You girls make the call to Edward Rose."

Data was watching the lobby television and fiddling with his laptop. He'd figured out how to surf the Internet while hooked up to his cellphone, and was now able to go on-line from wherever he happened to be.

Travis wasted little time explaining. Data, of course, wasted no time catching on. "Is there anything you could hide in the padding of a helmet that might be used as an explosive?" Travis asked.

"Give me a minute," Data said.

Data's good hand flew over the keyboard. The screen flickered with images as he worked through search engines. He stopped, went back a page, nodded, and then turned the screen toward Travis, Nish, and Fahd.

Data had found something that looked, to Travis, like a piece of squashed Silly Putty on a table. His grandfather had once given him the toy, soft pink plastic that came in an egg. You could roll it in your palm to make different shapes, bounce it, or roll it along a comic book to take a perfect imprint of whatever was on the page.

"Silly Putty?" he said.

"Not Silly Putty," Data corrected, "C4 – plastique. The most dangerous explosive known to be in the hands of terrorists."

They were still staring at the screen when Sam and Sarah came bursting out of the elevator.

"We got him!" shouted Sam. "He checked. He says it looks like someone tampered with his, too."

"Who?" Data asked, his head turning.

"Edward Rose. He's on his way over here. He says his helmet is the same as Nish's. Somebody fiddled with the padding."

"But none of this makes any sense," said Fahd.

"It makes perfect sense," Travis said, "if you want to blow up the Queen of England."

"Why would anyone want to do that?" Fahd asked.

"Guy Fawkes would," Travis said. "And today is his day."

Travis wished he had a better mind. He wished he had a processor up there instead of a bunch of brain cells that didn't seem to have all the right connectors running between them.

He told them about overhearing the cellphone call by the Serpentine. The others thought at first, as Travis had, that Mr. Wolfe calling himself "Fox" was no different from his calling the Screech Owls "Barn Owls" – that he was just another absent-minded Englishman – but when Travis suggested it might be code and Wolfe might not be his real name either, they began to follow him.

Mr. Wolfe was using "Fox" as a code name – and today was Guy Fawkes Day.

Guy Fawkes had tried to bring down the British government with explosives, and now the royal family was headed to the Tower of London.

Mr. Wolfe/Fox had spent the night in the Tower with the Owls and the Young Lions.

Mr. Wolfe/Fox/*Fawkes*? had given out the helmets, and *insisted* they be taken into the Tower the previous evening.

Both helmets had mysteriously vanished, then reappeared – but someone had tampered with them.

"Oh, my God," said Sam.

The revolving doors spun round and Edward Rose, his long hair flying and helmet in one hand, came running into the lobby.

"I was at my aunt's," he said. "I was only two Tube stops away. What's going on?"

They explained as best they could, Edward Rose's eyes growing wider with every unbelievable claim.

"I knew from the start there was something about Mr. Wolfe," he said. "He seemed to know nothing about in-line skating. And we couldn't understand why they were going to all this effort."

"He did it to get access to the Tower," Sam suggested. "That's why we're here. Made it an international 'event' and was able to get the Tower for a sleepover because it was just kids from the Commonwealth. You know, a goodwill gesture."

"Some goodwill," Travis said, "if he plans to do what I think he's doing."

"Call the police," Fahd said.

"And tell them what?" Travis asked. "That someone's planning to blow up the Queen with the insides of a hockey helmet? They'd think we were nuts. *We have to have some proof!*"

"We can test it," Edward Rose said.

"Test what?" asked Travis.

"Test the helmets for explosives. They have those machines all over. You know, the ones they have at the airport-security lines to check computers and carry-on bags for explosive materials."

Travis knew exactly what he meant. Travis, after all, had carried Data's laptop into the Tower for him and had gone through exactly that test.

"Does that make sense, Data?" Fahd asked.

"I think so," Data said. "Plastique is almost impossible to detect, but those machines would find it if anything could."

"But it's gone!" Nish cried out. "Someone's already taken it out of the helmets. What would be the point?"

"Residue," Data said. "The machines check for residue. That's why they wipe them and then check the cloth. They only need the slightest trace to indicate that someone was handling explosives."

"Where would we find one?" Travis asked.

"We'll go back to the Tower," Edward suggested. "We know there's one there."

"*Hurry!*" Travis pleaded with the group. "*We haven't much time!*"

17

IT WAS EDWARD ROSE'S IDEA TO TAKE THE TAXI. The centre of London was thick with crowds gathered to cheer the royal family, and the streets along the procession route had been closed to all traffic.

"If a London cabbie can't get us close," he told them, "no one can."

They had pooled their money and Travis was carrying it. He had no idea how many pounds he had in his hands, but he hoped it would be enough.

Five of them went: Nish and Edward Rose with their helmets, Sam and Sarah and Travis. A full load for a London cab.

The first two taxis parked on the corner of Nutford Place, just outside the hotel, refused to go anywhere near the impossible traffic of central London on the day of a royal parade. The third, however, was intrigued. He was smoking a cigarette when the kids came to his window, and Edward Rose handled the negotiations.

"A hundred quid if you can get us there in twenty minutes or less," Edward Rose said.

The man blew smoke in Edward Rose's face. Travis didn't like the look of the driver and wanted to move on, but Edward Rose stood his ground.

"A hundred quid," he repeated.

"You ain't got that kind of cash, sonny," the man said.

Travis held out his hand. He had no idea if he was holding a hundred pounds, or two hundred, or fifty – he didn't even know what a quid was.

The driver grabbed his cigarette and tossed it into the road. "*Let's go!*"

They piled into the back of the cab, three of them stuffing themselves into the comfortable rear seat, Travis and Sarah pulling out foldaway seats facing backwards. All strapped themselves in with seatbelts.

Travis was glad he was firmly buckled up, and equally glad he couldn't see. The cabbie drove like a madman. He squealed around corners, flew through red lights, darted down alleys so narrow Travis was convinced the paint was going to be raked off on both sides, tore the wrong way up one-way streets, and almost flew down the bigger roads when he could find an opening.

The twisting and turning was beginning to make them sick. Nish had gone completely white, a colour rarely seen in his big tomato of a face.

Sam was hanging on for life to Edward Rose's arm – though Travis had the strangest feeling she'd have the same grip on his arm if they were stopped dead in a traffic jam.

Edward Rose called out the landmarks as they hurtled through London toward the Tower.

"Gower Street, good . . . there's Lincoln's Inn Field . . . Newgate . . . St. Paul's Cathedral . . . We're almost there, gang."

"I'm almost gonna hurl . . . ," Nish said, now beginning to turn a little green.

"Hang on," Edward Rose said, laughing. "Only a couple more minutes."

The traffic was snarling. The police were turning back cars. Barriers were up everywhere. The crowds were thronging toward the river and the Tower to get as close a look as possible at the royal procession.

"Close as I can get yer, mate," the cabbie said. "I count twenty minutes."

"Good enough," said Edward Rose.

"One hundred quid, please," the man said, lighting a new cigarette.

Edward Rose helped Travis count it out. There was plenty. They jostled out of the cab, Edward Rose turning to thrust the money in at the man.

"There's your money," Edward Rose said. "But don't spend it all on cigarettes – your smoking will kill you faster than your driving will."

"Ah, get lost," said the cabbie, wrenching his cab in reverse and pulling away.

"Charming!" Edward Rose said. "But he did his job. We're here."

They had to push their way through. A lot of the people, especially the ones who had begun lining up at dawn, resented what they took to be pushy kids trying to make their way closer to the front. They were cursed and called names, but they didn't dare stop. They apologized as much as possible, though it didn't always work. One red-faced gentleman even took a swing at Nish, who crouched in the nick of time and duck-walked through a row of tall men just in front.

"*There's security!*" Sam called back to them. "*It's just ahead.*"

There were barriers ahead to keep people back from the entrance to the Tower, and the crowd was standing six deep behind it.

"We have no choice," said Travis. "We'll have to barrel through."

They dropped their shoulders and began pushing harder, trying to apologize to everyone at the same time. The ruckus caught the attention of the police, who were gathered in a circle around several motorcycles and a horse-mounted police officer, quietly talking while they waited for the procession to begin.

The police hadn't expected a scene like this. The royal party still hadn't left Westminster Pier and it would be quite a while yet before the procession reached the Tower. A huge policeman with a curling moustache grabbed Nish by the scruff of his neck and hauled him bodily out of the crowd.

Nish's helmet slipped from his hand and went skittering across the road. Several people in the crowd laughed.

Travis was grabbed by another policeman and Edward Rose by a woman officer. The two girls broke through and over the barrier and stood, waiting.

"We need to see someone in security," said Edward Rose.

"You're looking at him, boy," said the policeman holding him by his arm. "Talk."

"We think someone took explosives into the Tower last night. We were part of the group that stayed over. We think someone tricked us."

The bobbies looked at each other.

"Was there kids here last night?" the one with the curling moustache asked.

"Yes," said the woman officer. "Some group from Canada, I think."

"That's us!" Sam and Sarah yelled at the same time. "We need to see someone who can check these helmets."

"For what?" said the cop holding Travis.

"Plastique explosives," said Travis.

Suddenly, he had everyone's attention. The moustachioed bobby let Nish drop onto the pavement and all went quiet. Even those in the crowd who had been shouting at them went quiet.

"Where?" the policewoman asked.

"In the helmets," said Edward Rose.

"*In the helmets?*" the large policeman said, looking at Nish's dropped helmet as if it might go off.

"Not now," said Travis. "Someone used the helmets to sneak the plastique into the Tower and then removed it once they were inside. We think there might be residue."

The policewoman understood immediately. "You youngsters come with me."

The woman police officer led them past more barriers, more crowds, and more police to a security base outside the main entrance. Travis sighed with relief. The explosives detector was still there.

The policewoman explained quickly. Men in plainclothes moved in and took the helmets from the two boys, and a technician took out the plastic wand with a small cloth wrapped around its tip, which she traced all over the inside of Edward Rose's helmet.

She removed the cloth, placed it in the machine, and pushed several buttons. The machine closed on the cloth, whirred, and lights flashed.

"Maybe," she said. "But it's not a very strong reading."

She took Nish's helmet and performed the same procedure.

The machine whirred and stopped. A red light came on and stayed on.

The technician looked up, fear in her eyes.

"I have a reading for plastique," she said.

18

TRAVIS WAS ASTONISHED BY THE EFFICIENCY. In a matter of minutes the police had cleared the entire entrance to the Tower of London and were moving the crowds back down the street. The people were remarkably obedient and moved almost silently, the only sound a murmur of confusion as they tried to figure out what had happened.

It was clear, however, that they all understood there had been a security threat. They knew what that could mean, thought Travis. They knew everyone had to work together. He couldn't imagine people behaving in such an orderly way back home.

The police took the five youngsters to a security tent and had just begun interrogating them when a senior officer came in and said that they would have to evacuate.

Sirens began wailing. A television was playing in the corner of the tent and Travis saw that there was confusion everywhere.

"The BBC has learned of a security breach at or near the Tower of London," an announcer came on to say. "We will have details for you as soon as we know them ourselves. There has been no incident – repeat, no incident – but a security alert has been sounded and evacuation is under way in the immediate vicinity of the historic Tower."

The police loaded the five friends into a police van and, with sirens screaming, headed up Tower Hill and away. The roads were blocked everywhere, grim-faced bobbies directing all traffic away from the area,

"We'd better be right," Nish muttered. He was looking ill again.

The morning papers were filled with the story:

"400-YEAR-OLD-PLOT FOILED AGAIN!" said the *Mirror*.

ATTACK ON ROYAL FAMILY PREVENTED," announced *The Times*.

"GUY FAWKES PLOT FIZZLES!" cheered *News of the World*.

The gift shop in the Screech Owls' hotel seemed to have hundreds of copies of dozens of different papers, all with their front pages dedicated to the story about the astonishing plot.

Mr. Wolfe was a phony. There was no Mr. Wolfe, and there was no International In-Line. The plotters, a terrorist group with so-far undetermined connections, had apparently spent millions of pounds – "quid," Nish kept saying – setting up their false front for the attack. The ingenious plan was concocted purely to get the rare plastique explosives into the Tower without being detected. The organizers knew they could never carry it off themselves, but a bunch of kids just might.

"Mr. Wolfe" – his real name was still unknown – who set up his headquarters near Wembley Stadium, had seen the Young Lions practising in-line hockey, which gave him the idea for his outrageous plan. Another plotter owned a sporting-goods store, which New Scotland Yard police suspected was a money-laundering operation for a terrorist group believed to be involved in the illegal drug trade. It was an easy step to supply the team with new equipment, complete with false International In-Line logos and labels.

The Crown Jewels celebration, if not the actual details, had been known for more than a year. It was assumed the Queen, and possibly the entire royal family, would be journeying to the Tower of London for the special commemorative ceremony on November 5. That the celebration would coincide with Guy Fawkes Day was a happy coincidence for the plotters. It is believed this is why the main organizer took up the name "Mr. Wolfe." A wolf might succeed where, in 1605, a "fox" had failed.

Mr. Wolfe had reasoned that plastique could be smuggled past security at the Tower of London if it were carried by innocent-looking kids. The plotters had inquired early on to see if the Young Lions team might be given special entry to the Tower, but the request was turned down on the basis that, if it were done for one British team, it would have to be done for others. The staff at the Tower did not wish to set a precedent.

So Mr. Wolfe, on behalf of International In-Line, took out advertising space in *The Hockey News* and ran his contest in Canada, the nation known for inventing the game of hockey. An exception could be made for some special visitors, and who would ever suspect a bunch of twelve- and thirteen-year-olds from Canada?

The Screech Owls of Tamarack were selected in the contest and the plot was quickly put into action.

A novel way of getting the explosives inside the Tower still had to be found, and so was born the idea to give two of the players new helmets as awards for their play, and to insist that they bring along the prizes for the sleepover. The guards would understand; the explosives would make it in the entrance; and the plastique would be removed by the plotters, who were posing as International In-Line executives.

Before being hidden in the Jewel Tower, the explosive could then be attached to a cellphone and rigged up to be triggered by a call made just as the royal family entered.

And it might have worked but for Travis Lindsay's long run around the Serpentine and his mind double-tasking while he wasn't even aware he was thinking.

That part, Travis knew, he would never be able to explain.

Nish was furious that the Owls had all agreed to say as little as possible about their curious role in the unravelling of the plot. Travis had wanted it that way. So, too, had Edward Rose, who turned out to be as far from a vain, full-of-himself hotshot as Travis could have imagined.

Travis wanted nothing said about what he'd done. He'd only been a small part of it, in his mind. Data had figured out the explosives. Edward Rose had got them to the Tower in time. The policewoman with the explosives detector had found the traces that led to the evacuation and discovery of the hidden plastique.

"What about *me*?" Nish kept saying. "I wouldn't mind being interviewed."

"You didn't do anything except almost throw up," countered Sam.

"It was *my* helmet! I'm the one who discovered there was something wrong with it!"

"Think about it, Nish," said Sam. "If your head was any bigger you'd never have noticed anything."

Nish blinked. "But . . . but . . . but . . . ," he began, not quite sure what Sam had said, but knowing that somehow it *did* make sense. "I guess you're right," he said, sighing deeply.

It was an historic moment, Travis thought to himself with a smile.

The world's biggest peewee publicity hound had admitted defeat.

19

"THERE'S NO GAME," SARAH SAID.

They were in the lobby of their hotel, and she had just got off the telephone with Edward Rose, who had called the moment he heard.

Mr. Wolfe and his phony associates had made no effort to book Wembley Stadium for an in-line hockey exhibition. That was why there had never been coverage of the big event by the BBC or by any of the London newspapers. Mr. Wolfe had known all along there would be no need.

But the game had meant everything to the Owls. It was why they had come. It was what they'd been working toward.

Muck came into the lobby, whistling. "The game's back on," he said. "I just talked to the Young Lions' coach."

"At Wembley?" Fahd asked.

Muck shook his head. "No. At the Serpentine. Best we can do under the circumstances — but we're still going to play for the World Cup of In-Line Hockey.

"How can we do that?" Andy asked.

"Simple," Muck said, smiling. "No one else does it. So it's whatever we say it is."

"Maybe this is *better* than Wembley," said Sarah. Her voice cracked. She was shaking.

Travis was shaking, too. Not from the cold – it was an unseasonably warm day for November in London – but from the tension, the anxiety, the *excitement*.

Thousands of people had come to Hyde Park and gathered near the Serpentine to watch the first-ever, instantly invented World Cup of In-Line Hockey.

A reporter from the *Mirror* had found out more about the Screech Owls' part in the biggest story of the year. She had not got all the details – she knew nothing about Travis's guesswork and the frantic ride in the London cab – but she knew that the Owls had been tricked into carrying the deadly plastique into the Tower of London, thereby endangering their lives as well as the lives of the royal family.

And she also knew, because Mr. Dillinger had slyly let her know, that the Screech Owls had also been duped into coming over for a major event that never was to be.

"The kids," Mr. Dillinger had told her with his droopiest sad-faced look, "have had their dreams shattered."

Her story had run on the front page, and now it seemed everyone in London wanted to cheer on the Screech Owls from Canada and watch this so-called World Cup of In-Line Hockey – it had been Mr. Dillinger's idea to tell the reporter that as well – played against the Young Lions from Wembley, who had also been unfairly used by the evil plotters.

The story had captured the imagination of a city grateful that a terrible deed had been foiled – even if no one knew exactly *how* it had been foiled.

As if by magic, people began walking along the paths of Hyde Park and Kensington Gardens and assembling near the outdoor in-line rink a half hour before game time.

"There are several hundred people out here!" Mr. Dillinger had announced, giggling, sticking his head in through the tent flaps of the makeshift dressing room.

A few minutes later he was back.

"There are *thousands* of people out here!" he announced, his moustache dancing as he snorted in delight.

The Screech Owls were getting more and more nervous. Travis was shaking so hard he felt as if he'd just stepped out of the water at his grandparents' cottage after staying in too long.

Mr. Dillinger's head appeared again. "*There's more than a million!*"

"Oh my God!" Sam screamed.

Mr. Dillinger grinned. "Just kidding – but there *are* thousands. With more coming."

"This is horrible!" wailed Fahd.

"This," said Nish, "is what I *live* for."

"We don't even know how to play!" said Sam in despair.

"We know how to play," said Sarah. "We just have to remember what we practised."

The Owls continued dressing. Shaking, Travis pulled his jersey over his head. He remembered to kiss where the "C" should be as it passed over, and his heart jumped when he realized, looking out from inside, that good old Mr. Dillinger had now sewn it on.

He pulled the jersey all the way on and checked the others. Sarah had her "A," and Nish had his.

Data, too, had an in-line jersey on, even though he wouldn't be playing. And he, too, had an "A."

Just then the tent flaps parted and Muck walked in, a chuckling Mr. Dillinger right behind him. Muck moved to the centre, stood there for a moment, and turned completely around on his heels until he stopped, staring intently at Nish.

"Don't say a word," Nish said, his face beaming. "I know exactly what to do."

"It's what we *don't* want you to do that I worry about," said Muck.

Nish said nothing, just resumed his usual pre-game position of crouching over his legs and trying to bury his face into his knees.

Muck looked around. "This game doesn't mean a thing, as everyone here is perfectly aware," he said. "So it matters only as much as you want it to."

He stopped, stared around at the players looking up at him, their eyebrows all but forming question marks.

Then he left, abruptly, and without another word.

Derek started giggling. "What the heck was *that* all about?"

No one knew.

But then Nish, who usually never said a word before stepping out onto the ice, suddenly stood up and slammed his stick down.

"*I want to win!*"

Sarah stood, also slamming her stick.

"*I want to win, too!*"

Suddenly all the Owls were on their blades, sticks pounding in a haphazard circle.

The game mattered, Travis knew.

It mattered a great deal to them all.

20

EVERYTHING FELT DIFFERENT.

Travis had his stride. His in-line skates felt, for the first time, as if they were just part of him, his skin and bone, not some contraption tied onto his feet. This was the way his ice skates felt when everything was going just right. He hadn't expected it so soon with the in-line skates.

He hit the crossbar on the first practice shot.

He didn't feel small like he did last time. He looked up the playing surface toward the Young Lions, also warming up, and they didn't intimidate any more.

He saw Edward Rose, also with a "C" on his jersey, his golden hair flying out the back of his helmet. He watched him hit the crossbar and pump his glove in the air.

Travis laughed. He had the same superstition!

Travis was circling near centre a moment later when he felt a sharp rap on his shin pads. He looked up. Edward Rose was smiling at him. "Have a good one," he said.

"You, too," Travis said back.

Nish was deep in concentration, stretching in the corner, not even lifting his head to look at the other side. Wayne Nishikawa, all business. The way Muck liked Nish to be when the big games were on the line.

Travis looked beyond him.

His heart almost stopped.

They were pushed against the boards as deep as he could see. Perhaps thirty rows back. Men in dark suits, a few even wearing black bowlers. Woman smartly dressed for business. Young people in jeans.

Television cameras!

There were people there by the thousands, and they were even cheering the warm-up.

How long would they stay? Travis wondered.

Would they be disappointed?

They stayed.

They stayed and watched and cheered for nearly two hours as the Screech Owls of Canada played the Young Lions of Wembley for the World Cup of In-Line Hockey.

This game was not an 8-1 rout. This was a *game*.

Nish was a demon in his own end, hitting the Lions and freeing up the ball and stepping around checkers to send long feed passes up the boards.

Travis had his legs and he had his wind and it seemed, suddenly, as if he finally had a game to play. The plastic ball stayed on his stick better this time. He seemed to have more time, more confidence.

Sarah, playing on the other wing, was all grace and speed, handling the ball beautifully and passing perfectly.

But Dmitri was the one who put Muck's game plan into play. It was he who first circled back on a rush, who swung left and then curled back, holding the ball and drifting it back to Nish, who sent a nice lateral over to Fahd, who then dropped it once again to Dmitri, still cruising back.

The play seemed to confuse the Young Lions, who had been quickly backpedalling in order to deal with Dmitri's recognized speed. They reacted as Data had predicted. They waited and then they charged ahead, chasing the ball carrier.

The moment Dmitri realized that the Young Lions had gone into transition, he dug in himself and burst in the other direction toward the Young Lions' goal.

The Wembley team tried to react, but their wheels couldn't catch on the hard plastic surface the way sharp blades – *Mr. Dillinger* sharp blades – could on ice, and by the time they turned to deal with the reverse of flow, Dmitri and Sarah and Travis were in on a three-on-two.

Sarah read it perfectly. She let Dmitri and Travis charge the goal, Dmitri carrying, while she set the triangle. She would be "late man in," even though she was a twelve-year-old girl. It was the way everyone described the play, and she kind of liked it.

Dmitri flipped to Travis, and Travis neatly tapped the ball back into the slot, with Sarah at the top of the triangle coming in fast as the defence split, one taking Dmitri, the other trying to ride Travis off into the corner.

Sarah faked the shot, cupped the ball in her blade, and curled around the falling goaltender to slip it, gently, into the back of the net.

Owls 1, Young Lions 0.

The first lead, ever, in Screech Owls in-line history.

"Nice goal," Edward Rose said as they lined up to face off again.

"Thanks," said Sarah, blushing deeply.

Then, on a beautiful solo rush that caught Wilson flat-footed, Edward Rose tied the game. The Owls came right back, Lars now taking over ball control and weaving back and back until he had suckered the Lions into chasing.

The moment the chase began, Lars hit big Andy Higgins on a break and Andy simply overpowered the Lions' goaltender with a huge slapshot.

Owls 2, Young Lions 1.

They were hanging in. They were not only hanging in, they were ahead.

The crowd loved the action. It was fast. It was end-to-end. And there was plenty of scoring, something that made this sport different from soccer, no matter how similar the attack patterns.

Heading into the final period, it was Screech Owls 5, Young Lions 4. Travis had scored on a lovely feed from the swift Dmitri, and Jesse had scored an impossible goal when he punched the ball out of mid-air and it went like a line drive right through a crowd in front of the net.

Edward Rose had scored three of the Young Lions' goals and set up the fourth.

"Win or lose," Muck said before the final period began, "you've made it matter. I'm proud of you all – even you, Nishikawa."

Nish didn't even acknowledge the rare compliment. He was in "win" mode – just the way Muck needed him for the third period.

Travis looked up at the makeshift clock Mr. Dillinger and the Young Lions' manager had hung on the side of the closest dressing room.

Two minutes to play.

Game tied, 7-7. Dmitri had scored with a backhand that had knocked the bottle off the Young Lions' net. Simon had scored with a neat tip on a Nish shot from the point. And Edward

Rose had five goals and had set up the other two.

It was now Dmitri's line against Edward Rose's line.

Travis scanned the crowd. Not only had no one in the crowd left, there seemed to be thousands more, all cheering equally for the two sides. Travis couldn't believe they would do that. One side was home, the other from across the ocean, and yet they were being treated just the same.

He could see one of the men closest to the boards collecting money. They were betting on the game.

Edward Rose led a great rush up the floor, only to be stonewalled by Nish's big hip knocking him off the ball. Nish took it himself, heading straight up like a steamroller. Travis raced to keep up on the wing, his stick down and ready for a pass.

Suddenly Nish went flying as a blur of red jersey moved in and swept the ball in the other direction.

Edward Rose – where had he come from?

Edward Rose had only Sam back. He turned her inside out with a shoulder fake and a tuck, moved in on Jenny, faked her down to her back, and pinged the ball in off the crossbar.

The crowd went crazy!

Young Lions 8, Screech Owls 7.